Secrets of a Lady

Isabelle Montclair

CONTENTS

CHAPTER 1

Cool grey eyes summed up the situation ahead in one glance. A tall man in black evening dress stood in the narrow street fending off what looked like two – no three, footpads. His drawn sword was keeping them at bay for the present, but for how much longer? Even as he stood there, two of the footpads started working together to engage the sword with their sticks while the third angled in to strike a blow at their victim. The watcher could hear the tall man gasping for air as his sword flashed furiously trying to defend himself from three sides at once.

Rather reluctantly, the watcher realised he would have to go to the aid of the man under attack. Moving quickly once he had reached that decision, he drew a small silver pistol from his right hand coat pocket and levelled it carefully at the nearest assailant. The sudden explosion startled all four men and the nearest footpad clapped a hand to his arm, blood spurting between his fingers. Four heads swivelled wildly seeking to discover the source of the attack and he shouted excitedly, "Quick after them, Jack, we'll see some sport tonight!" In a flash, the would-be robbers deserted their prey and fled down the street.

The watcher waited a minute then stepped out of the shadows and towards the other man who stood still, holding his sword and breathing heavily.

"My thanks to you, sir, whoever you are, and to your friend. That was a good shot in poor light." The only light in fact came from the moon and all that he could see of his rescuer was a dark slight shape of medium height. His dress however seemed that of a gentleman and his voice confirmed it.

"T'was my pleasure, sir," He bowed slightly, "Although as you see, I'm afraid I invented my friend for the occasion!"

"My house is nearby. Perhaps you would permit me to offer you a drink? My name is Carleton by the way, Richard Carleton," the man in evening dress introduced himself. He held out a hand and his rescuer shook it.

"Peter Francis," he offered, a little hesitantly it seemed.

"You'll join me for a drink then?"

"Well ..."

"Just for a few minutes," Carleton interrupted, heading off a refusal. "Or would it not be convenient?" This last was said rather coolly and the younger man realised that to decline the invitation would appear churlish.

"Thank you, that would be very pleasant," he gave in gracefully.

He fell into step beside the other man and seemed to be concentrating on keeping his footing amongst the cobblestones. After several minutes silence, Carleton inquired pleasantly, "Have you been in London long, Francis?"

"No, only a week. I – I've been abroad."

"Doing the Grand Tour?"

"I'm afraid not. I've spent the last three years living in Italy, and several years in France before that."

Carleton wondered whether it was just his imagination, but each answer from his companion appeared to be carefully considered before being spoken – almost as if he were making them up as he went along. However a few readily answered questions about Rome and Florence soon proved he had certainly spent some time in both places. Perhaps he was merely reserved. "And that is something I can surely sympathise with," Carleton thought wryly to himself.

Ten minutes walk found them at the house he had rented for the Season in Grosvenor Place and they went up the steps. The door was opened by an elderly butler and Peter followed Carleton inside. He stood blinking in the bright light while the butler removed his master's coat.

"Bring some claret to the study will you, Rawlings? This way," he gestured, turning to the other man. Seeing him properly for the first time, he saw that his "rescuer" was much younger than he had supposed, surely not more than eighteen or nineteen. He had fair hair, cropped short in the prevailing fashion, steady grey eyes, a smooth skin browned by a foreign sun, and a firm, though slightly rounded chin. He was dressed neatly, if not expensively, in dark blue coat and pantaloons with a white cravat at his throat. He wore no jewellery except for a signet ring on one slim hand.

Peter on the other hand, saw a tall man of perhaps thirty with rather harsh features under his dark curly hair. He was dressed, as he had noticed earlier, all in black which accentuated the thinness of his build though, as his swordplay had shown, it was the thinness of whipcord. It was also apparent that his host belonged to a much higher level of society than himself. His coat was exquisitely tailored and must have cost more than Peter had spent on clothes in his entire life.

At the same moment, each became suddenly aware he was sizing up the other. Peter's lips twitched and he laughed. "I'm sorry, sir," he quickly apologised and after a second Carleton smiled back.

"Claret?" he offered as Rawlings poured two glasses from the bottle and then set it down on the study table.

"Thank you, sir" Peter took the claret and sipped it appreciatively.

"Seeing as you saved my purse, if not my life tonight, I don't think you need to call me sir."

"Thank you ... " Peter looked a little self conscious.

Suddenly at a loss for conversation, Carleton asked, "What was your favourite place in Florence?"

"The Duomo, of course," Peter mentioned the famous cathedral. "But to be honest, I really enjoyed the art collections. There are so many masterpieces, the Uffizi alone is simply marvellous." His guest's eyes had lit up with true enthusiasm. His eyes went to the painting on the wall in front of him, surely it was a Canaletto? "You are interested in Italian paintings yourself, I see?"

Carleton confessed that he was, and also in Italian sculpture, and the two men talked for over an hour. Carleton revealed at one stage that he had made the Grand Tour himself some years ago but that his companion was more interested in sport than art. "Well I enjoy sport as well of course but ... in Italy! My companion couldn't see any point at all in staring at a lot of dusty old portraits. Nor could my father, which was why I was landed with someone so incompatible for my guide!"

"What a shame! Have you never thought of going back yourself then?" queried Peter.

"Frequently, especially when I get fed up with the Season and its endless gossip!"

Peter laughed and took out his watch. "I'm sure I must have been here for ages. Good heavens! It's after one o'clock, I hope I haven't outstayed my welcome."

"By no means. I haven't had such an interesting conversation for a long time." Carleton rose to his feet reluctantly. "Shall I see you at White's?"

Peter shook his head, exclusive London clubs were above his touch.

"I'd be happy to sponsor you if you'd care to join," Carleton offered.

"That's too good of you!" Peter looked up in surprise, Carleton knew next to nothing about him. Then he realised that the offer had been made in part to repay him for the assistance he had given that evening. "However, I don't think I'll be mixing in such circles this visit – I- I'm not particularly plump in the pocket at present," he explained further with a touch of embarrassment.

"I see. Well the offer still stands, there's no need to play the tables you know."

Peter merely smiled and inclined his head.

"In that case, I'll bid you good night," replied Carleton a little stiffly. "Shall I get you a hackney?"

"No thanks, it's just a short walk."

"May I ask where you are staying?"

Peter hesitated a moment then named the Pelican, a modest inn some couple of miles north. "I'm sorry, I don't want to impose on you."

Carleton made a noise which in a lesser man would have been called a snort and saw his guest to the door. "Till later then".

They shook hands and Peter strode off into the night – so much for lying low in London! Still he'd had no choice but to help Carleton and he'd enjoyed his company very much. If things had been different they might have been good friends.

John would be waiting up for him – it was very late, perhaps he'd better take a cab after all. He found one at the next corner, having just unloaded a passenger, and soon he was rattling over the cobblestones at a brisk pace.

Carleton went thoughtfully up the stairs to his room. There was an odd air of secrecy about Francis – apart from his taste in art, he knew nothing of him after their conversation other than his name. What was his background? Where did he come from? Was he even English for that matter? Despite the mystery he rather thought he liked him.

CHAPTER 2

A short, thickset man with the unmistakeable air of an old family retainer was waiting in his room when Peter opened the door. The single candle had burned down to within an inch of the holder but the coals still glowed in the grate. "Well, and what have you been up to then?" growled the retainer, coming forward to help him off with his coat.

"Don't scold, John" protested Peter half smiling. "I've had such an adventure! I came upon a man being attacked by three footpads and I had to lend a hand. And then he wanted to thank me and we got talking and I forgot the time ..."

Far from soothing the servant this information only seemed to aggravate him further. "Don't tell me you went to this man's lodgings? On your own? Who was he?"

"Yes, I did. Don't worry I was quite safe. His name is Carleton, Richard Carleton - have you heard anything about him?" Peter went behind a screen as he spoke and draped his garments over the top as he took them off.

John stayed in the centre of the room, glaring into the fire. "No, I can't say ... no wait a minute. I think the family has a place in Surrey. Don't know where he fits in though - but it's not right, you visiting him at home, whoever he is!" he protested, returning to his original theme. "And this ain't seemly either," he muttered to himself as he gathered up the clothes ready for cleaning.

"You should be used to it now, John - God knows I am!" came the slightly weary voice. "I'm too tired to talk any more about it tonight - Good night, I'll see you in the morning."

"'Night, Miss Frances," came the soft reply and then the door shut behind him.

Frances sighed and stretched. Gad it was good to be out of that binding. Dressing as a man had become harder as her body grew decidedly female. She fell into bed with a final image of a pair of thoughtful brown eyes under unruly black hair lingering in her dreams before she was soundly asleep.

Frances had spent more of her twenty four years as a boy than as a girl. Her mother had died before she could really remember her and since then, she and her father had travelled throughout Europe, spending no more than a few years in any one place. She knew Frances was her Christian name but she didn't know her surname - she had had at least a dozen different ones over the years and did not know which, if any, was the name she had been born with. Henri Fayette (Paris) or Giuseppe Monteverdi (Rome) had been quite simply an adventurer as long as Frances could remember.

Her father had lived by his wits and his skill at cards. His fortunes however had fluctuated and many had been the time that it had been safer for Frances to be a son rather than a daughter. Her education had been as varied as the places she lived in. She could speak French and Italian like a native, her German was not quite as good, but as well as these permissibly feminine accomplishments she could shoot and fence and ride without a side saddle.

It had been a devastating shock when her father had fallen ill a few months back and died in their lodgings in Florence. When he had finally realised the seriousness of his illness, in fact the very day before he died, he called Frances to him. "You must go to London ... find Julia Murray - Lady Julia, she'll see you right. Just tell her, Henry Metcalf ..." a fit of coughing had prevented him from finishing. He gripped her hand tightly and whispered his last words to her. "Remember, Lady Julia Murray ... give her my ..." Another bout of coughing shook him and he lay back exhausted against the pillows.

After his death, Frances had numbly made the funeral arrangements, paid their bills, packed her two trunks and set off to England with their manservant John Hopgood for her sole companion. She had automatically chosen her male garb for the journey as it made everything so much easier, and faster. A single woman could not put up at a respectable inn without a female companion or travel by herself in a carriage.

When she eventually landed in England, she saw no reason to abandon her disguise. "Peter Francis" had therefore travelled to London by coach from Dover and booked into the Pelican with the minimum of fuss. Her plans were to lie low while she located Lady Julia Murray and find out what she could about her. Frances had no intention of throwing herself upon the charity of a perfect stranger. She had enough money from their last gambling venture to allow her to live in a moderate fashion for several months.

She had planned to live quietly in London for several reasons other than money however, not the least of which was her desire to be unrecognised should she have the opportunity to become a woman again. Although she had every confidence in her disguise, she realised that a close friend of Peter Francis would remark audibly on his replacement by Frances. She would just have to stay away from Richard Carleton.

The next day was bright and sunny, a fresh breeze blowing a couple of small white clouds about the blue sky. As Frances strode briskly through Hyde Park, she wished rather wistfully that she didn't have to live quite so quietly. The theatre for instance - how she would love to see some English Shakespeare! There was so much happening in London at the moment, plays, operas, balls. For the first time in her life she thought it would be fun to be a young girl enjoying a London season, dancing and flirting the nights away. She sighed. It would also be very pleasant to hire a horse and ride in the Park - perhaps her purse would stretch to that once or twice during her stay.

She really must get a move on and find this Lady Murray. It was difficult to know quite where to start. She had no acquaintances in London to ask and her tentative enquiries at the Pelican had not borne fruit. She had taken to buying a paper and looking through the Society news, but so far she had had no luck. What she had noticed though was a short column about a masked ball that was being held by Lady Dalrymple in three days time.

Lady Dalrymple was one of the season's foremost hostesses commented the paper, and the occasion was sure to be a sad crush. Unbidden, the thought had slipped into Frances mind that surely, in such a sad crush, one more person would not be noticed? And how better to find out about Lady Julia than at a ball where the gossip buzzed like a swarm of bees? Perhaps she could even ask someone to introduce her? But the risks! What if she were caught trying to get in the house and was taken up for a burglar? The idea continued to tease her however and she was still deep in thought when she heard her name called. "Francis?"

Startled, she looked up into the amused face of Richard Carleton. At the same time she realised that she had left the Park and was now making her way down Oxford Street. She blinked and smiled, "My apologies, sir, I was daydreaming".

"Sound asleep more like!" joked Carleton. "Are you on your way to anywhere in particular? If not, perhaps you would like to join me at Mancini's Fencing Salon? He has a new thrust he has promised to show me."

Frances' eyes lit up. "That would be fascinating, I accept with pleasure, sir!" Only then did she remember, too late, her vow to steer well away from Mr Carleton! Oh well she mused philosophically, I'll just have to avoid him tomorrow. They turned off Oxford Street shortly and soon found themselves climbing the steps to the two upstairs rooms where M. Mancini conducted his fencing lessons.

He was a short, dark-eyed Italian and Frances heart gave a sudden lurch of fear that she might have met him in Italy before she realised he was a complete stranger. He came quickly forward to greet her companion, hand outstretched. "Ah my Lord Carleton, you have come to learn the "kiss of death" yes? And your friend? I have not met him before I think." The inquisitive brown eyes were turned directly on Frances and she gazed steadily back, masking the jolt his use of "Lord" Carleton had given her. A Lord? She should definitely have avoided his company.

CHAPTER 3

She bowed in the Italian style and introduced herself, "Peter Francis, Maestro." The eyes lit up. "You speak Italian? Have you learned your sword play there as well?"

Rather reluctantly, Frances nodded. "I had a few lessons with Maestro Ricardo." Surely it would do no harm to mention this? It was the truth after all and one of the first lessons for an adventurer was to stick to the truth as often as possible!

"Ah ..." Mancini looked at her with interest. "Perhaps when I have finished the lesson with Lord Carleton, you would care to...?" He broke off as Frances shook her head.

"I'm sorry, Maestro," she said, flushing a little. "I'm afraid I cannot afford lessons at the moment."

Mancini looked a bit taken aback then said enthusiastically, "No matter. This time there is no charge because I would like to see something of how the great Ricardo teaches". Frances bowed to inevitability and accepted the offer, inwardly fuming at her own recklessness which had led her to accompany Carleton in the first place.

Carleton regarded her quizzically, "You have hidden depths, Francis."

"So do you, 'my Lord'", she retorted.

"Come, come," urged Mancini, "Let's start, my Lord".

Carleton took off his coat and selected a buttoned foil. "En garde". The two men went quickly through a series of warm up movements before they began fencing in earnest, Mancini occasionally commenting on his noble pupil's performance. "Higher there, my Lord ... well done ... no! wait til I am fully extended before you try that one ..."

Frances watched interestedly, her gaze moving from one man to the other. Mancini was obviously the professional. He moved with practised precision, his wrists as flexible as India rubber and his speed sometimes almost faster than the eye could see. Carleton on the other hand was a good amateur, who was strong in defence and quick in attack. He gave a good account of himself and twice got a blow through Mancini's guard.

Frances began to prepare herself for her own bout to come, taking deep measured breaths and flexing her knees and wrists. She watched closely as Mancini demonstrated his "kiss of death" to Carleton. It involved an orchestrated clash of blades at a certain angle and then a carry on thrust to the throat. It reminded strongly of a manoeuvre Ricardo had taught her, although she thought hers might be trifle neater.

All too soon the men were saluting each other and Carleton was moving to one side, wiping the sweat off his brow. "Your turn, Francis."

Outwardly calm, she moved forward to select a blade, forcing herself to think solely of the techniques she would use and to think of nothing else beyond the next ten minutes. They were more evenly matched for height and weight and their eyes met across the blades raised in salute. Mancini went through a similar set of preparatory exercises as he had with Carleton and Frances followed his lead carefully, conserving her strength.

"Right, let's see what you can show me," invited the Italian, breaking off momentarily. Frances nodded and let him take the lead again, content to defend herself and bide her time. After a few minutes she detected a slight restlessness in her opponent and a moment later she recognised the opening move of his "kiss of death". She met him blow for blow, then, as he made the final thrust, she twisted her own blade up in a curious motion that sent Mancini's sword flashing up past her shoulder, and landed the button of her own foil at the base of his throat.

"Magnifico!" breathed the astounded teacher. "How did ...? No keep on ... later." The bout continued but the Italian was now on his guard. Frances had used most of her strength and concentration on achieving her initial success and struggled to hold her own. Mancini soon had his blade against her heart and she surrendered breathless but smiling.

"I must crave your pardon, Maestro, and stop there." He looked rather incredulous and she trotted out the explanation she had used in the past. "As you can see, I have some skills but alas not the strength to follow them up. I had the wasting sickness when I was a lad and my limbs have never gained full strength."

"What a shame, young sir!" he exclaimed in dismay. "With more practice, you might have become a master - Ricardo taught you that trick?" Frances nodded. Mancini continued to shake his head regretfully.

"Perhaps you'd have a turn with me sometime, Francis?" enquired Carleton from the wall where he had been watching curiously.

"If you like... but I'd be no match for you, my Lord, your arm is too strong," she replied casually.

"I must say you're cool enough about it," he commented, his expression unreadable.

"I have no choice sir! However it doesn't affect my shooting. I'll wager I could meet you equally enough with pistols!" Thinking he was taunting her, Frances answered rather hotly.

"Steady on, young Francis, I meant no offense," Carleton laughed. "Though it would give me great pleasure to engage in a friendly shooting match with you - I have already had some evidence of your skill with firearms remember?"

Frances looked searchingly at him but could see no trace of mockery. "I'm sorry, my Lord," she apologised gruffly. She turned to Mancini. "I must thank you very much for your time maestro and bid you good day. I have an appointment in an hour and must get home to change now," she spoke in Italian. He returned her bow and shook Carleton's hand. "Next week as usual?" he queried and the other man nodded.

Once outside, Frances turned to Carleton. "I must be away, my Lord. Thank you for bringing me this morning, I have not fenced for some time and it was good to feel a sword in my hand again."

"I enjoyed watching you," he confessed. "You have a brilliant style for one so young."

"I had the best teacher in Maestro Ricardo," excused Frances, "and I started early. One does in Italy."

They walked in silence for a few yards, then Carleton spoke. "Would you care to meet me in Manton's Gallery for some shooting one day? We could have a wager as you suggested, a small wager, perhaps, between friends?"

Frances flushed, "I did not mean that."

"What, backing down?"

She glanced up and saw he was teasing. "I would not wish to rob you, my Lord," she answered demurely.

Carleton laughed, "Friday then? Are you free?"

Frances considered. That would be the day after Lady Dalrymple's masked ball. She nodded. "I shall see you there at … what time?"

"Two?" She agreed and they parted company. Of course she couldn't meet him Frances told herself, but it had been easier to agree. Certainly he would be offended when she failed to keep their appointment but at least that would make him unlikely to seek out her company again. Perhaps by Friday she would already be under Lady Murray's protection. The thought was not as cheering as she had expected.

She turned her mind to the masked ball. If she went, would she go as male or female? She'd be more likely to learn about Lady Murray as a woman of course … and it would be more fun … It was all nonsense, wishful thinking, naturally she'd spend the night quietly in her room as usual.

Carleton strolled back to his own house, his thoughts also turning to the Dalrymple's masked ball. Perhaps Rosamond would be there. At twenty nine, Carleton was still unattached, without even the mistress that most men of his class had on the side. He had found no-one yet that he wished to marry and was too reserved, fastidious even, to seek out a casual relationship which was distinguished, as he saw it, by lust on one side and avarice on the other. As far as the succession went, he had a cousin with a healthy young family, who could easily take over if he failed to provide an heir. Not that he had given up just yet! He still hoped to find someone who would share his interests as well as his bed, perhaps Rosamond was the one.

CHAPTER 4

On the morning of the ball, Frances was still considering whether to attend or not. Doubtfully she looked at her two dresses, one plain and deliberately servant like and the other a reasonably pretty morning dress with blue trim but definitely not a ball gown. "Well that settles that," she told herself firmly. However, when she found herself strolling down Bond Street an hour later, she realised her subconscious had not listened. She paused outside a particularly modish shop and made a bargain with herself. "Alright then, if there's a gown in there that will fit me, I'll buy it and go to the ball. If there's not, I won't."

Hesitantly she entered as befit a very young gentleman shopping for his mistress. Before she could get her bearings a saleswoman stepped up smiling, "May I be of assistance, sir?"

"Well I ..." Frances halted in well simulated confusion, "I'm looking for a dress - for my sister... it's for a ball." Despite the fact that no young lady she had ever known in her entire life had sent her brother to buy a ball gown, the assistant continued to smile. "I see, sir, and what size does m'selle take?"

"Eh? Oh I don't know ... she's nearly my size ... just a little smaller," her voice trailed away as the assistant beckoned her over to a fabulous creation of gold satin. Frances looked doubtfully at it. "I don't think I could afford anything as grand as that."

The assistant frowned, "I'm afraid we do not stock many ready-made gowns - most customers prefer to have them made up." She paused thoughtfully, then snapped her fingers for a young attendant. "The green one, from the back." There was a slight delay and then the girl reappeared carrying a green silk gown carefully over both arms. She held it up gingerly by the shoulders and Frances fell in love with it. Pale green, like shallow water, it was not suitable for a young girl but for a married woman. A trim of white lace around the neck and the puff sleeves set it off nicely.

"How much?" she queried fearfully.

"Two hundred guineas," came the rude awakening. Frances sighed and turned away reluctantly.

"That is," continued the saleswoman smoothly, "It was two hundred guineas originally when it was made for Lady Fairfax, however she changed her mind. Now it is only a hundred and eighty - pounds."

"I'll take it," the words were out before Frances could stop them. "I do not have the whole sum on me at present, but if I could pay half now, could someone deliver it to me at my room at the Pelican and I will pay the rest then?" This arrangement turned out to be quite satisfactory, in fact it was quite a pleasant change as many of Madame Lisette's customers delayed weeks before settling their accounts. Frances left her direction then set off with her head in a whirl. Now she would have to buy some slippers and some gloves, and a reticule and a hairpiece! At this rate she would have to win a very large wager with Carleton to keep living in London for more than a couple of weeks!

Turning her back on these thoughts, for now she was committed to attending the ball, Frances made her way to Grafton House, where she had heard that one could pick up the most amazing bargains. Sure enough, she found all the accessories she wanted there and even remembered at the last minute to purchase a black mask. Muttering bashfully about his sister's birthday, Peter Francis managed to complete his shopping in under an hour and for a mere ten pounds. Trifling when one compared it to the cost of the gown!

She summoned John immediately when she returned to the Pelican. "I need a carriage for tonight, John, a proper carriage, not a hackney. I am going to Lady Dalrymple's masked ball."

He stared at her open mouthed, "You're what?"

"I'm going to a ball, a masked ball. I've bought a gown and everything."

"You've gone mad!" was the flat reply.

"Well only a little," she admitted. "But I'm sure 'tis the only way I'll discover Lady Murray and besides I feel like being a woman again for a while."

"Are you invited?"

"Of course not! How could I be? I shall just have to bluff my way in - that's why I need a carriage to make an impressive entrance - how does Amelia Blenkinthorpe sound?"

"Unlikely!" returned her harassed servant. "No doubt you'll be turned back at the door," he assured himself. "And how do you think you're going to get out of here, all dressed up in your finery? Not to mention getting back in!"

"Hm ...," Frances nibbled a fingertip as she considered. "I think I could slip out while everyone was at dinner, if you were waiting for me with the carriage around the back. Perhaps I had better take my breeches and a coat with me in the carriage so I can change on the return journey. I shall make a point to leave at a quarter before twelve before the unmasking. Can you have the carriage waiting for me?" she asked, fleshing out her plan.

"Hmph! I can see you're set on it so I'll do my best about the carriage. You'd better hop to it if you want to be ready before midnight!" he remarked acidly as he left the room. Frances lost no time as she needed to do everything for herself, there was no maid to assist her! She was accustomed to being her own maid however, and when John returned to admit grudgingly that he had managed to hire a carriage, he found her already dressed and carefully powdering her face. No lady would have such ugly brown skin! Painstakingly she attached the dark brown wig to her own short locks, tucking any fair strands out of sight and then put on the black mask. She was totally unrecognisable as Peter Francis.

Smiling she met John's eyes in the mirror.

"You'll do," he approved reluctantly. "Have you got the garments you want ready? I'll take them along to the carriage now." She handed him the dark cloak, boots and a pair of breeches. "I'm ready. Is the carriage at the back of the inn?"

He nodded. "In that case, I will come down as soon as the coast is clear."

Frances waited until John had disappeared down the corridor, then, checking in both directions, stepped out of the room and shut the door behind her. Moving softly, she hurried after him, listening for the sounds of anyone approaching. Everything was quiet until she opened the door at the bottom of the stairs and noise from the taproom filtered along the passage towards her. She could imagine the scene, Will the landlord would be serving mugs of ale while Mary his wife would be in the kitchen preparing dinner for the two or three guests who regularly ate in. As she paused, a servant girl came out of a room ahead and disappeared into another.

Holding up her skirts, Frances slipped down the passage into the store room and out through the back door to the small courtyard and stables. John was standing at the head of a pair of horses attached to a smart looking coach with the door swinging open. She trod purposefully toward it, ignoring the startled exclamation of a stable hand coming out with a bucket of water, and climbed in. John shut the door smartly behind her, jumped up behind the horses and they were off.

CHAPTER 5

Frances allowed herself a quick sigh of relief. One hurdle had been cleared, now on to the next. Night had fallen by the time they drew up outside the residence of Lord and Lady Dalrymple. Burning torches lit the entrance and a steady stream of beautifully dressed guests were making their way in. She waited a few minutes as a large party got out of several coaches and reformed, laughing together, on the pavement.

In a flash she was out of her carriage and had attached herself to the rear of them. She followed them up the steps keeping just far enough behind not to attract their attention. She pretended to stumble on the top step and then hurried after them, with a petulant "Well, I do think you might wait for me!" Looking neither right nor left at the doormen, she passed unchallenged into the hallway.

Lord and Lady Dalrymple were standing just inside the doorway ahead to welcome guests, smiles fixed on their faces. Frances followed her camouflage party. Before her courage could desert her, she curtseyed to her hosts and said smilingly, "Tonight I am Diana, my Lord".

The rather portly gentleman before her looked a bit taken aback, then said gallantly, "A goddess, indeed!" and bowed her through to his wife. Frances curtseyed a second time and moved on without speaking again. She had done it! She was in. For a moment relief threatened to overwhelm her but she breathed deeply and soon found her way to the centre of the ballroom.

Almost immediately a tall Harlequin approached her for a dance and Frances found herself whirling around the ballroom. It was all very informal and she enjoyed herself immensely. After dancing for nearly an hour with several different partners, she remembered her primary purpose in attending. She disengaged herself with some difficulty from a young red haired Walter Raleigh and went looking for the powder room. It was upstairs and crowded as usual with young girls chattering about their admirers. On the pretext of pinning up a torn hem Frances sat down quietly in a corner and listened.

"Lord Henley has asked me to dance twice already ..."

"and I said I'd be delighted if only ..."

"Have you seen what Honoria is wearing?"

"Is the one all in black Jack Lambert do you think?"

Suddenly out of the medley of gossip, Frances heard a familiar name and she leant a little closer.

"Mama wishes me to accept Lord Carleton - if he offers for me, but he's so cold! I'd rather have someone lively and gay like Jack Lambert. You're so lucky, Amanda, although nothing has been announced yet has it?" The young voice added thoughtfully. The owner was a girl of perhaps eighteen, with golden curls, a pink rosebud mouth and large blue eyes, rather close set, thought Frances nastily to herself. She was exquisitely dressed in a pale blue gown and wore a string of pearls around her slender neck.

Her companion would have been considered pretty enough if she had been alone, but she appeared dull and ordinary next to the blonde vision. Brown ringlets framed her face and her pale pink gown was in the latest fashion. She was using her black mask as a fan and paused for a moment to reply confidently "No, nothing has been arranged yet but 'tis only a matter of time now mama says. After all it would be such a suitable match with his lands so near to Fenhurst."

"I find it difficult to picture Jack settling down to a quiet life in the country! What about his opera dancers?" exclaimed her friend.

"Really, Rosamond!" protested Amanda with a frown, "I don't know what you mean!" She put the mask back on her face rather forcefully. "Are you ready yet? We should return to Aunt Louisa."

Rosamond laughed and glanced quickly again in the mirror. "Yes, I'm ready. By all means let's find Aunt Louisa." The two girls went out together.

Frances continued to sew, her head bent down over her lap. She had almost finished when another young girl burst into the room holding a trailing hem above the floor. Grey eyes met blue and they both laughed.

"Men are such clumsy creatures!" exclaimed the new comer, sitting down beside Frances. "Oh you do sew neatly! I make such big crooked stitches, Sophie says a child could do better. It's only a little tear ... I don't suppose you would consider...?" her eager voice trailed off hopefully. Frances looked into an enchanting little face, framed with dusky brown curls setting off an enormous pair of blue eyes and a smiling mouth. Her lips curved despite herself and she nodded.

"Alright, I'll fix that for you if you like, at least so that it will hold for tonight. Perhaps we had better introduce ourselves. I'm Diana ... Diana Murray," she added with sudden improvisation.

"Oh would you? How kind you are! I'm Sammy Fairfax. Sammy is short for Rosamonda of all things but there are two of us this Season so I decided on Sammy. It's what I am always called at home and I like it much better anyway," she chattered on. "Sophie says it's not ladylike, which may be true, but I don't look particularly "boyish" do I?" she demanded archly, a dimple suddenly appearing in one cheek.

"No", agreed Frances, taking in the small but very female figure. "I think it suits you very well. I've finished here so if you would show me the hem which needs attention ..."

Sammy shuffled around and eventually located the tear. It was on the other side of her dress so she exchanged places with Frances who began to repair the damage. "This thread is not the same colour as your material," she observed, "So you will have to get someone to mend it properly for you when you get home."

"I'm very grateful - are you new in town? I don't think I've seen you before."

"Yes, I've just come up from the country for a short visit. Is this your first Season?"

"Oh yes. I've only been out two months. Everything is so exciting in London, isn't it? I don't think I've stayed home for one night in weeks! I want to live here for ever and ever and never go back to Surrey. Sophie says I shall have to find a husband who prefers London, but I don't think I shall want a husband for simply ages yet.

Sophie is my sister-in-law you know, she married my older brother Harry and I'm staying with them for the Season."

The name suddenly rang a bell and Frances queried, "Would that be Lady Fairfax then?"

"Yes, that's right. Do you know her?"

"No, only I think we go to the same dress shop! There, I think that should hold up for the rest of the night." She rose to her feet. Sammy jumped up and thanked her again. They left the room together, Sammy continuing to chatter away about the dresses she'd worn and the balls she'd attended, so that Frances felt she knew half of London society just from listening to her. During a brief pause for breath, she asked idly. "I believe I have a distant relation in London, Lady Julia Murray, do you know of her at all?"

Sammy frowned thoughtfully. "Lady Murray," she mused. "No I do not think I have met her. I could ask Sophie if you like, she knows everyone! Do come and meet her, I am sure you would get on famously!"

Frances hesitated, the knowledgeable Lady Fairfax sounded like someone she should definitely avoid, as she would certainly be much more interested in her background and credentials than the artless Sammy. She had a sudden inspiration, why not tell the truth? Or at least part of it. Her look of embarrassment was not wholly feigned.

"Another time perhaps ... you see the trouble is that this gown," she gestured at it, "was actually made for Lady Fairfax! She found it did not suit her but I just fell in love with it. However, you do see why I could not meet her while wearing it!"

Sammy looked concerned. "No, I do see that. Well, I shall ask her about your cousin myself and pass it on to you later." She smiled conspiratorily and they both replaced their masks and stepped out into the ballroom.

Sammy was immediately surrounded by a flock of young men, eagerly begging her for the next dance. She smiled happily at all of them, "No thankyou, Sir Thomas, I've danced with you already and you too, Jack, I mean Mr Lambert. What is the next dance by the way? Oh a waltz? Then I shall be pleased to accept you, Nick, you dance it beautifully." She was whisked away by a slender young man with bright red hair and freckles and Frances found that the man she had addressed as Jack Lambert was asking her to dance instead.

"I don't think we have been introduced yet, Miss ...?" he paused invitingly.

"Diana" answered Frances smiling saucily. She spoke with a slight French accent. "And I would love to dance, thank you m'sieur."

He looked at her with rather more interest and led her out onto the dance floor. Like many of the guests he had not come in costume but merely wore a black mask over his eyes. Jack Lambert was a tall well built man with broad shoulders and the well muscled thighs of an athlete. He was a little older than the other two men, perhaps nearer to thirty than twenty. Although he danced superbly, Frances thought that he would be more at home on horseback or even in a boxing ring. He held her firmly but impersonally and Frances enjoyed the sheer speed and movement of the dance, despite a wayward moment of speculation as to how Carleton would be to dance with. They exchanged a few idle commonplaces but Frances noticed the curiosity in his eyes as he studied her.

"Do I know you?" he asked.

"No, you haven't met me before," she said boldly. "In fact I doubt you will meet me again. I am just up to London for a short visit."

"Where do you come from, Diana?"

"Abroad," she replied.

He raised his eyebrows. "But you know Sammy Fairfax?"

Frances was silent as they spun neatly around a slower couple in their path, then said frankly, "No, I met her for the first time tonight."

"A woman of mystery indeed!"

She laughed, enjoying being able to hold his attention. She had noticed the blonde Rosamond staring at them from the sidelines and was pleased he hadn't glanced at her. Lambert watched the mischievous smile on her lips and said suddenly, "I have an odd feeling that you are not a respectable person Diana."

"No" she agreed, "I am an adventuress. Lord and Lady Dalrymple have never met me before and I just walked in off the street!"

For a second he almost believed her, then laughed at her joke. He recalled then that Lady Fairfax was a tall woman and also Sammy's sister-in-law by Jove. Perhaps it was her, that mask certainly concealed a lot of her face. "Forgive me," he answered. "I shall be anxious to see you again after midnight, per chance I will find I know you after all."

Frances just smiled demurely and he considered the possibility of setting up a flirtation with her, discreetly of course. The music finished at that point and rather reluctantly, he released her. Frances curtseyed and left him to go in search of a glass of lemonade. The time had flown and she should start to think about leaving shortly. Perhaps she could find Sammy after her drink and then leave, she mused. She found the bowl of iced lemonade in the supper room and was just about to ask a footman to serve her when Lord Carleton spoke beside her.

"May I be of assistance?" Frances started and was glad she did not have a glass in her hand as she would have dropped it.

"Thank you, m'sieur", she replied, emphasising her French accent to disguise her voice. "Some lemonade please." He looked very elegant she thought, in black ball dress with white lace frothing at his wrists and collar. He poured the lemonade for her and then a second glass. He gave the first to her with a brief smile then turned away to where Frances could see the blonde Rosamond seated against the wall. Not only did he not recognise me thought Frances ruefully, he scarcely even noticed me. She left the supper room sipping her lemonade and went in search of Sammy.

Sammy however was engaged in a country dance and she realised she would not be able to approach her about Lady Murray for some time. Avoiding Jack Lambert, who appeared to be searching the room for someone, Frances stepped back into the supper room for a glance at the gilt clock on the sideboard. Half past eleven, time to go she decided. Making her way casually through the crowded ballroom, she had just stepped into the hallway when Sammy dashed up to her.

"You're not leaving already, Diana?" she protested.

"Yes, I must. My companion is waiting, she is not feeling well," Frances prevaricated.

"Oh, I am so sorry ... but I asked Sophie about Lady Murray as I said I would, and she said the only one she knows is an old lady who lives very retired these days, but her name is Anna not Julia so I don't know if she is your cousin or not."

Frances untangled the sense of this and queried "An old lady? Do you know how old?" To a girl as young as Sammy, forty could appear "old".

"Yes, around seventy, Sophie said."

"Perhaps she has a daughter?"

Sammy's face fell. "I didn't think of that ... but wouldn't she be called Lady Julia instead of Lady Murray?"

Frances nodded as her young friend continued. "I will ask Sophie and let you know next time we meet."

"Thank you, Sammy, I shall call on you one day soon," Frances promised, then hurried out to meet her coach feeling like Cinderella.

John was waiting with the coach across the road, and she hurried over so as not to keep the horses standing too long. He opened the door for her, shut it firmly, then climbed up into the driver's seat and sent the pair trotting over the cobblestones. Inside, she drew the curtains and changed awkwardly out of her gown and into the boots and breeches. At the last minute she remembered to pull off her wig and wipe the powder off her face. Clutching the cloak about her, she left the coach a couple of hundred yards from the Pelican and walked the rest of the way while John trotted past her to return the team to the stables.

Frances reached her room without attracting undue attention. Carefully she sponged off a couple of small stains then packed the gown out of sight at the bottom of her bag along with the slippers and gloves. It would never do for a chambermaid to see them lying about. "What a night," she said to herself yawning. "I enjoyed dancing with Jack Lambert and I liked Sammy. I do not think much of Rosamond whatever-her-name is though, a nasty little cat. Carleton could do much better for himself surely. I hope he is not too taken with her."

Gentle snores greeted John when he came in later to check on her, and he left as silently as he had entered.

Meanwhile, back at the ball, Jack Lambert searched unsuccessfully for a tall lady in a green dress. Eventually he approached Sammy. "Where is your friend Diana?" he asked as casually as he could.

She turned wide blue eyes on him. "She went home before midnight. Why?" she asked saucily.

"None of your business chit!" he grinned at her. "I'd like to call on her, can you give me her address?"

Sammy frowned suddenly, "No I am afraid I can't, I'm sorry but she didn't tell me."

He raised an eyebrow.

"It's true, Jack. I met her tonight for the first time, and somehow it didn't come up in the conversation."

"You only met her tonight?" he asked, half incredulous.

She nodded vigorously. "Yes, she helped me with my gown. All I know is that her name is Diana Murray and she is visiting London from the country." Lambert was about to question her further, still half believing "Diana" was Sophie Fairfax playing a joke, when Lady Fairfax herself came up to Sammy. She was wearing a blue gown and he saw immediately that her eyes were brown and not grey and that her mouth was a different shape. He bowed hastily and withdrew, his mind seething with conjecture.

Carleton was dancing for the second time with Rosamond Lyle and thinking how pretty she was. It was a pity she was so shy, she seldom had much to say to him. Perhaps he could take her driving one day and he could gain her confidence. Rosamond thought about Jack Lambert.

CHAPTER 6

Bright sunshine woke Frances later than usual the next morning and she suddenly remembered she had an appointment that afternoon with Lord Carleton at Manton's pistol gallery. She hadn't been intending to keep the appointment, but now she reconsidered. She did not yet know enough about Lady Murray, or her circumstances, to allow her to make any decisions as to her future. However, what with Peter Francis being acquainted with Lord Carleton and Diana Murray becoming fast friends with Sammy Fairfax and Jack Lambert, her future was looking complicated to say the least!

She dressed hastily in her male attire and went down to breakfast. A quick mental calculation of her remaining funds persuaded her that she would soon need an income. Perhaps she should take up Carleton's offer to introduce her to his club and she could try to win a few guineas! A moments reconsideration warned her how risky that would be, and she put aside the idea regretfully.

Peter Francis sauntered out of the Pelican shortly after noon and made 'his' way through the narrow streets towards Manton's gallery. She loved walking in London, looking at the shops and stalls and the wide variety of people all going about their business, maids scurrying on messages, busy housewives buying cloth to take home and sew into sturdy waistcoats or pretty dresses, and of course young men of leisure wandering between entertainments.

Carleton was already there when she arrived, waiting outside the building. He smiled to see her and greeted her almost as an old friend. He led the way, pushing open the heavy door which allowed the noise of pistols exploding and men shouting to rush out into the street. She followed him inside and along a corridor, past a room filled with unruly men, and into a larger, quieter, gallery obviously reserved for the upper classes. On the far side, a young man of about twenty was practising rather erratically, watched by an attendant with a bored eye, but otherwise the room was empty.

Playing cards were set up near the far wall in various patterns as targets and several weapons were displayed in a locked cabinet near the door for the use of those patrons who had not brought their own. Carleton was carrying a box with two duelling pistols in it. He opened them up for Peter's inspection. "I had them made for me here in London. What do you think? Would you like to try one out?"

Frances picked up one of the pistols with interest and balanced it in her hand. "Nice," she murmured appreciatively. She held it at arm's length, pointing it down the gallery towards the targets and taking aim. "Yes, I'd like to try one of these, my Lord." Carefully she replaced it in the box and looked at him.

"But we are competing are we not? In which case I would prefer to use my own. I only have one I am afraid but you are very welcome to use it if you would like to." As she spoke, Frances took a smaller silver plated pistol from an inside coat pocket and handed it to him to inspect. "It's Spanish" she explained.

"It feels very light," Carleton commented dubiously.

Frances smiled confidently. "One does not need a cannon to hit the ace of spades, my lord, you'll see." She paused, "Are you a good shot?"

A little taken aback by her directness, he demurred, "I'm considered a fair shot I believe."

"Well in that case, as our wager is between friends, shall we say five guineas, my Lord?"

Carleton frowned, a little offended, "You sound as if you expect me to lose!" he retorted.

Frances smiled deprecatingly, "Well, you see, I am considered an excellent shot. I wouldn't want to take advantage of our friendship!"

He regarded her a moment through narrowed eyes, then laughed. "I'll be damned if I know what your lay is, youngster. By all means let it be five guineas if you wish - I'll take you to dinner on it! Best of three?"

Frances nodded and carefully loaded her pistol "After you, my Lord."

Carleton loaded both weapons, then chose one and stepped forward to the white line painted across the floor. Put on his mettle by Frances self assurance, he took his time between each shot and placed one hole in the centre and the other two edging the black of the spade.

"Rather better than fair, sir," remarked Frances drily.

Watched by a satisfied Carleton and an interested attendant, she took careful aim with her silver pistol and fired off three shots in quick succession, only pausing to reload in between. Carleton saw the single hole in the black and said bracingly, "That one is in the centre at least, not bad for a first attempt."

Rather to his surprise, Francis looked very pleased with himself, unable to keep a little smile from his lips as he turned to the attendant. "If you would be so good as to bring the card up here?" The man went willingly and Frances looked with slightly guilty apology at Carleton.

"I am sorry, but when one shows off, it is so good to succeed!" The attendant gave her the card and she passed it to Carleton who held it up to the light. He could see then that the hole was a fraction larger than that made by a single bullet - the youngster had scored three bullseyes in a row! He pursed his lips in a low whistle, "Excellent shooting! Well done, lad!"

Frances flushed at his praise, "There are only two things that I do well, my Lord, and that is one of them! May I try your pistol now?" Carleton nodded, still impressed. With an unfamiliar weapon, Frances hit wide of the spade at her first shot and clipped the edge of it at her second. "I find it a little heavy after my own. I'd need to practice to be as accurate with it."

She turned back to Carleton to find that he had been joined by a couple of well dressed gentlemen in buckskins. One was a stranger to her but the other was her dancing partner of the previous night! She fancied he was looking rather closely at her and bent down to return Carleton's pistol to its case.

"May we join you, Richard?" Lambert was asking. "Harry has a new pair he wants me to try, claims they are the best he's handled."

Carleton nodded, "Have you met Peter Francis? Jack Lambert and Harry Belmont." They all shook hands. "Harry rather fancies himself as a good shot too, Peter - you two should have a match," Carleton continued slyly.

Frances shot him a look of reproach but Belmont said eagerly, "What a capital idea!" He reminded her of a young puppy, full of bounce and enthusiasm. Already he was unpacking his precious new guns and running through their points, oblivious that no-one was really listening.

"What will it be?" Lambert asked Carleton, "Best of five? What about the five of spades then?"

"What's the wager?"

Men, thought Frances crossly to herself, everything had to be a wager. "I can't afford more than a few guineas" she spoke up firmly.

"That's alright," Carleton stepped in smoothly. "I've a hundred here that says you'll win."

Lambert grinned "Right then, here's another hundred that says he won't. No hard feelings I hope, Francis, but I've seen Harry shoot before."

"Who will go first?"

"One after the other? A shot at a time?"

The two rivals agreed rather dazedly to their sponsors' arrangements. Carleton noticed the serious look on Peter's face and said cheerfully, "Don't worry, lad, it's not your money!" Frances scarcely glanced at him, that's what was making her nervous.

Harry grinned across at her and fired his first shot into the black of the top left spade. Frances aimed carefully but nerves got the better of her and the resulting hole was at least half into the white. The other man relaxed a fraction and hit the next spade but not quite as neatly as before. Frances shook her head, took two deep breaths to relax her concentration, and shot straight into the centre of her target. Harry followed up with another three good shots but Frances interspersed each with a perfect centre. The attendant went down to the end of the room to collect the cards while Frances and Harry waited anxiously.

Lambert and Carleton studied the two records closely. "What do you think? This one is a bit out but all the others are dead on target. These are close, though not completely in the middle - bad luck, Harry," Lambert concluded eventually, "but I think Francis has beaten you. Here, see for yourself."

Belmont glanced at the cards then said generously, "Yes indeed. The first shot was obviously a slip. Damned fine shooting, Francis." He held out his hand and Frances shook it firmly, flushing a little with self consciousness.

"Good of you," she murmured. She offered her pistol for his inspection. "Like to try?"

He took it with interest and for the next few minutes they exchanged avid information and ideas on what made the best weapon, Harry agreeing that hers certainly seemed to have a true line.

Carleton looked at the two heads close together with an odd twinge of jealousy. Nonsense, he told himself, the lad's got a right to more friends than just you. He took the money Lambert was cheerfully paying out with some satisfaction - it was a while since he had got the better of Jack in a sporting venture.

"Here you are, Peter, half of this should be yours," he handed him fifty guineas and smilingly ignored his half-hearted protest. The four of them spent a further half hour at the pistol range practising and trying to persuade Francis to show them some trick shots. Eventually Lambert remembered that he was engaged for dinner that night on the other side of town and had to leave. Belmont also made his farewells after extracting a promise from Frances to meet him at the gallery again the next day.

CHAPTER 7

"**A**re you free this evening?" queried Carleton. "I'd thought of attending the opera. I haven't arranged a box so it would be just in the pit. Are you at all interested in accompanying me?"

Frances considered the idea and thought that should be safe enough. She smiled at him, "Thank you very much, I was just thinking the other day that I should attend at least once while I am in London. What time should I meet you there?"

They arranged to meet at the theatre, then went their separate ways, Frances heading to the Pelican for an early dinner and Carleton to his house to finish some business letters. Frances found she was looking forward to the evening and thought she could very easily grow accustomed to this way of life. The money she had won today would allow her to stay comfortably at the Pelican for some time longer. It was all very well, she chastised herself, but she should be attending more seriously to her future.

What would she do if Lady Murray could not be found, or more likely, refused to have anything to do with her? 'Peter Francis' could hardly live at the Pelican indefinitely. Perhaps I could set up my own pistol gallery, she joked, tucking in to a large plate of roast beef and potatoes.

She took extra pains with her dress that evening, putting on her best cream pantaloons and dark blue coat. Shiny black boots completed her ensemble and she brushed her hair carefully into the fashionable Brutus style. She stared at herself in the small mirror. A pretty enough boy b'Gad, perhaps she would not put Carleton quite to shame. She collected her gloves and cane and took a hackney to the theatre. There was a great crowd milling around out the front and it took her some minutes to locate Carleton, standing against the wall in his black evening dress.

"Evening, my Lord," she greeted him, pushing through the crowd. "What are we seeing tonight?"

"Ah there you are. It's by Mozart, The Marriage of Figaro."

"Wonderful, I saw that performed in Salzburg several years ago," she enthused.

They went in and found seats in front of the private boxes, along with the more wealthy tradespeople and gentlemen with less than respectable female companions.

Unattached young bucks sauntered back and forth eyeing the audience until the opera started and they could ogle the dancers. Carleton gazed at them with resignation, "One of these days, every-one will be made to keep quiet and listen to the singing," he joked. Despite the constant chatter around them, Frances enjoyed the first act immensely. The Countess was particularly good, though the Count could have been a bit stronger.

At interval, Carleton announced that he was going to stretch his legs and Frances accompanied him, wondering if they would ever find their seats again. From up in the second row of boxes, a man glanced idly down. He had sleek dark hair, olive skin and a certain feline grace which defeated his attempts to look English. He caught sight of the pair below and froze into immobility. His companion looked curiously at him. "Anything the matter, Comte?"

With a start the other man recollected himself, "Nothing. I just ... thought I saw someone I knew."

"A friend of yours?"

"No," the Comte realised he had been more adamant than he wanted and smiled without humour, "Can you tell me the name of the man in black? And his companion?"

"Who ...? Oh I see. That's Lord Carleton in the black but I don't know the name of the boy with him - a nephew perhaps?"

"Oh well it is of no consequence," the Comte dismissed the matter with a flick of his fingers and settled back in his chair. "Can you tell me the name of that delightful young lady over there?" He changed the subject smoothly and his companion was happy to oblige, finding it much more interesting. He hadn't liked the look in the Comte's eyes a few moments ago and he half thought he might drop Carleton a word of warning.

Meanwhile Carleton was saying casually to Frances, "There is a young lady I wish to pay my respects to, do you care to accompany me?"

She nodded and followed him up the stairs and along the corridors full of chattering patrons to whom this was the prime purpose of the evening, and eventually to the curtained entrance of the box he sought. She paused outside a moment to ascertain that Sammy Fairfax was not inside, then entered discreetly on seeing that the party was made up of strangers apart from Rosamond Lyle and her friend from the ball.

She was secretly amused by the appraising look Rosamond gave her and even more so when the judgement appeared to be favourable. Carleton introduced her to a matronly lady in puce satin who proved to be Rosamond's Aunt Louisa, and to her stout husband. With a tender smile he continued, "And this is Miss Rosamond Lyle and her cousin Miss Amanda Marlowe." Frances bowed politely to each of them.

While Carleton was obliged to exchange courtesies with the older Lyles, Frances addressed herself to the two cousins. "And how do you find the opera?" she asked innocuously.

Amanda confessed that it was very pretty and Rosamond said with an air of assumed sophistication that it was all very well but that she preferred a play. When pressed as to her favourite play she chose Hamlet but could offer no reason other than it was vastly tragic. Wickedly, Frances commented that the death of Othello must soften the hardest of hearts. Rosamond's agreement to this piece of fiction confirmed her opinion that she really knew very little about it.

At that point Carleton entered the conversation and Frances found herself fending off exploratory questions from Mrs Lyle about her circumstances. Fortunately, a chance reference to Italy brought Mr Lyle into the conversation with a heated diatribe against all foreigners and Italians in particular. Mrs Lyle and Frances were soon reduced to muttering noncommittal noises as Mr Lyle got into full stride of what was obviously a favourite hobby horse.

Her eyes attentively on the reddening face before her, Frances let her ears concentrate on what Carleton was saying to Amanda and Rosamond. From the odd words she could make out they seemed to be talking about the ball to be held soon in Rosamond's honour and the gown she was planning to wear. Not too soon as far as Frances was concerned, the interval ended and the visitors had to return to their seats.

On their way down, Carleton asked offhandedly, "May I ask what was your opinion of the young ladies?"

"I thought them both pleasant enough", returned Frances, seizing the opportunity to cast a few stones, "perhaps a little empty headed as very young ladies often are."

"Empty headed?" queried his companion stiffly.

Feigning ignorance of Carleton's special interest, she continued blithely, "Yes, Miss Lyle prefers plays to opera and her favourite is Hamlet because it is so tragic and Othello dies so sadly."

"But Othello does not even appear in Hamlet!" protested Carleton inadvertently. "I daresay she confused the names, Ophelia is fairly similar sounding," he defended belatedly.

"Perhaps," agreed Frances cheerfully, obviously more interested in finding if their seats were still empty.

Carleton looked and felt slightly ruffled.

"I am sorry if I offended you," his companion apologised with a smile, "At least she did not say the opera was pretty as her cousin did!" This made him laugh and they settled down to watch the rest of the opera in harmony with each other.

On their way out at the end of the performance, Carleton was accosted by an elegantly dressed man who stepped out in front of him from the crowd of patrons streaming out of the theatre, "What have you been up to, Richard?" he queried jovially, "Have you stolen the Comte's mistress?"

Taken aback, Carleton exclaimed, "What the devil are you talking about, Tony? What Comte?"

"The Comte Duverne. He was sitting with me and looked as if he had bitten into a lemon when he saw you."

Carleton shook his head, "Never heard of the man in my life - I assure you, Tony. Must be mistaken."

"Well you know best, but he asked me your name. Be on your guard, he is not someone I'd want after me!" Tony clapped him on the shoulder.

Neither man appeared to notice that Frances looked quite ill with shock. She bent down and pretended to adjust the buckle on her boot while she got some colour into her face and grappled with the news. The Comte Duverne was in London! She threw a fearful glance around the room, half fearing that he was even now bearing down on her.

CHAPTER 8

Tony took his leave, and Carleton turned back to Frances. "Alright?" he queried, curiously.

She nodded, offering no explanation, and after a second he continued walking.

"Care to come back with me for a drink?" he invited over his shoulder.

She felt she could do with a strong brandy at the moment but it would be beyond rash to go alone to Carleton's house with him a second time. "That is very kind of you, my lord, but -"

"Come now, I'll brook no refusal!" the older man interrupted smiling, "The night is still young ... unless there is some reason why you no longer want my company?"

Frances stopped in her tracks, her eyes flying to his face. Did he suspect? She had not seen that hard look in his eyes before, she did not think he had guessed her secret but he obviously suspected she was hiding something from him. She stiffened, squaring her shoulders, "I am sorry, my lord. It's rather that you may no longer want my company." She bowed slightly, "I'll go."

Already regretting his sharpness, Carleton put a hand on her shoulder, "Please don't. I apologise. I would very much appreciate it if you would tell me your full story, or as much of it as you feel comfortable in telling."

When he smiled at her like that Frances felt that she would have walked on coals rather than lose his regard. What was another risk to her reputation after all? It was already beyond redemption if her secret was discovered. "In that case I accept your kind invitation."

They took a hackney cab, as Carleton had not thought it worthwhile to bring his own carriage. The thought crossed her mind of the absolute impropriety of the action if she had been dressed as a woman. Men had so much more freedom.

In his study, with the coals stirred up into an orange blaze, Carleton poured them both a glass of brandy and asked, "Will you tell me what is between you and the Comte Duverne?"

Frances gaped at him. He smiled wryly at her, "You looked as sick as a dog when Tony asked me about him and I know I have never met the gentleman."

"I ...er," she stuttered.

"Tell me to mind my own business if you like," he offered, withdrawing slightly.

"No it is just ... well ... oh the devil! I'll have to tell you now or you will be imagining the Lord knows what!"

Carleton relaxed at this rather ingenious outburst and sat down.

"I'd rather not have told you," Frances confessed, "as 'tis not a pretty tale and you will only have my word for the truth of it. It was a gaming matter. I was in Paris at the time with my ... my father, and we visited a rather infamous gaming den. The Comte Duverne was there also."

Her mind went back to the scene, the smoke filled room, the Comte with a party of friends and hangers on, obviously the leader of the group and equally obviously half primed, and ready for a lark. His eyes, searching for diversion, had landed on Frances, a young boy as he thought, sitting idly at a table by himself watching the game across the room. He had risen to his feet and approached him. "A game of piquet, lad?" he enquired, seating himself without waiting for an invitation. "Just a friendly hand or two while I wait for my friends to finish their game."

"I tried to decline, but he was insistent," she continued. She had not tried very hard, she admitted to herself. She had been playing cards ever since she could remember. Her father had taught her originally so that he could have someone to play against and keep up his own skills, and then when she had shown such natural aptitude, so that she could join him in his livelihood.

After the first game which she suspected he had let her win, the Comte had insisted on increasing the stakes, no doubt thinking to frighten the lad out of what wits he had for cards, and then to have some fun with him when he couldn't settle the score. Frances, or Louis Caron as he had been at the time, had responded nervously but with some dignity and accepted five francs a point.

She looked at Carleton, "He thought he had found a pigeon ready for his plucking, but I play piquet well enough to know how to minimize a poor hand and make the most of a good one. The Comte became infuriated with my cautious wins and plunged more and more wildly. In addition I was not drunk nor had I sycophants to impress ... anyway the long and the short of it was that by the time he overturned the table in a fit of rage, I was 500 francs ahead!

He could not accept that I had beaten him and accused me of cheating. Luckily there was a witness who took my part."

She remembered the mixture of fear and excitement churning in her stomach as she had calmly faced the Comte and denied his accusations. Her father had been standing nearby to offer her protection if she needed it but not so close for anyone to think they were connected. Suddenly, the Comte had flung the money down on the table in a pretence of unconcern so as to maintain face with his friends and she had left shortly afterwards.

"Unfortunately," she continued, "the Comte witnessed our departure as my father was getting into our coach and gave chase, swearing that we had cheated him. My father, you see, was the witness to our game."

She looked up and met Carleton's questioning eyes, flushing. "I swear to you we did not cheat! But I admit we were there to make money if we could." She broke off and sprang to her feet. "It sounds damnable when I put it into words, doesn't it! How could I expect anyone to believe me? I'll understand if you wish to drop our acquaintance."

"But I do believe you, and I do not wish to drop our acquaintance," Carleton's low, measured voice stopped her at the door.

She turned and faced him, frowning, obviously he had not understood what she had said. "Your pardon but perhaps I was not clear - we were gamesters, 'twas our profession."

He nodded gravely, "Yes, I gathered that. May I ask what happened to your father?"

"He took ill in Florence, and died several months ago. I settled our affairs and came to London, although I have lived most of my life in Europe my parents were born in England. I thought it was time to come home," Frances explained truthfully.

"My sympathy on the loss of your father," offered Carleton sincerely. "Do you know what part of England he came from? Perhaps you have family here."

"Perhaps," agreed Frances. She hesitated to say anything further, she had already trusted him with more of the truth than she probably should have.

Rather to his disappointment, Carleton could see that Peter's confidences were at an end. He broke the slightly awkward silence.

"I don't mean to interfere, but if you need any help, come to me."

Frances summoned up a shaky smile, "You are too kind, my lord, I don't deserve your friendship."

"Nonsense, I like to make up my own mind about a man." He sought for a way to break the tension and added with a smile, "You have warned me quite clearly not to play cards with you, but perhaps we could have a game one day, just for the fun of it?"

"Of course, my lord," Frances smiled and stepped forward to shake his hand, "I should go, good night, sir."

Carleton made his way up to bed mulling over their conversation. There was something engaging about Francis, despite his shady background. He was no green youth himself, and was well aware of the different strategies used by men on the edge of society to attach themselves to the wealthy. But if Francis was one of those, he had certainly gone about it in an unusual way! He could not believe he had made his acquaintance deliberately. He could not have known Carleton would be attacked that night as he was passing - could he? Thinking back, Francis had tried to withdraw, several times in fact. It had been he, himself, who had pursued the friendship.

He felt suddenly a little uncomfortable, he did not normally befriend such a young man, but Francis did not act young, he must surely be older than he looked. He could hardly ask him his age at this point!

CHAPTER 9

Meanwhile, Frances had returned to the Pelican and was telling John that the Comte Duverne was in London.

He looked simultaneously worried and relieved, "Well that'll put an end to your gallivanting about town at least! You'll have to stay here while he is in London."

She sighed rebelliously. "I could still go out as Diana Murray!" she said with sudden inspiration.

Her servant rolled his eyes heavenwards. He shook his head as he took her boots out with him to clean, that was not even worth a reply!

Frances kept to her room for as long as she could bear it the next day, which was in fact only until she remembered her arrangement to meet Harry Belmont for shooting practice that afternoon. Feeling only slightly guilty for worrying John and keeping a careful eye out for the Comte she sallied forth to the pistol gallery and spent an enjoyable hour or so with her newest friend.

On her return to the Pelican some hours later, she was met by the innkeeper's wife, wringing her hands and alternately excusing herself and foretelling disaster. The gentleman had seemed so respectable, foreign of course, but she had had no idea he was going to turn out to be a murderer so she had let him sit in her best parlour to wait and then Sally had come screaming down the passage and Will had raced straight up and found Mr Hopgood crumpled on the floor as white and still as-

At this point the bewildered Frances realised something had happened to John. She grasped the woman's arm, giving her a little shake, and begged her to tell her quickly where he was and what had happened. She looked up at her somewhat affronted.

"That's what I've been telling you, sir! He was struck down by this foreigner, white as a sheet he was. We've put 'im to bed and sent Joe for the doctor. Doctor's here now, you can go up and see 'im if you'd like to."

"Yes indeed." Frances followed Mrs Cobb up the stairs, she was still talking though rather breathlessly as she climbed. "Hit on the head, my Will says. And such a fancy coat he had on too, I'd never have thought it. What d'ye think he was after, sir? I couldn't see anything missing from your room, not at a quick glance that is. I'll expect you'll want to see for yourself." They reached the door of John's room which was next to Frances' and entered after a soft knock.

The doctor, a middle-aged, harassed looking man with spectacles was just about to take his leave. He turned to face them questioningly, clutching his black case.

"How is he, doctor?" asked Frances anxiously.

"Concussed - not too badly I don't think, but he'll need to stay quietly in bed for about a week and then take things easily for a while. He'll need nursing for the first two or three days. I can recommend someone if you like. It will cost you a few shillings but Mrs Brown is better than most."

"Thank you, doctor, I'd be very grateful," Frances paid his fee and took down the name and address of the nurse. John was lying pale and still under the blankets but the doctor assured her there was nothing she could do but let him rest. Frances arranged with Mrs Cobb to have the nurse fetched, then suggested they go downstairs for a glass of sherry while she told her what had happened.

It appeared that a man had come to the inn just as dusk was falling, and asked to be directed to the room of Peter Francis. Although he was foreign, he was so well dressed and ever so politely spoken, that she had felt no hesitation in giving him the information. She had put him in her best parlour to wait for his return, and Will had taken him a bottle of burgundy which he'd ordered and left him to it.

The villain had then apparently crept upstairs and somehow attacked Mr Hopgood. The door to Frances' room had been ajar and the unconscious servant lying inside, so that one could only assume that the villain had broken in and been lying in wait for either Mr Francis or Mr Hopgood. After the brutal attack, the stranger had returned to the parlour, then come out as bold as brass to announce that he could not wait any longer.

Mrs Cobb marvelled here at the cold callousness of a man who could act so calmly after such villainy. As for describing him, he was dark, large of stature and had evil looking eyes. The landlady was so carried away with the excitement and horror of the event, that Frances did not think her identification could be relied on. She herself had no doubts that it had been the Comte Duverne, waiting to revenge himself on Louis Caron. Somehow John must have taken the blow meant for her.

Eventually she persuaded Mrs Cobb to return to the kitchen and went back to her room to try and think what to do. Her first thought, to call on the Bow Street Runners, was dismissed immediately. She was in no position to invite investigation, nor was there any proof that the attacker had indeed been the Comte Duverne.

One thing was certain, John would have to stay put at least for the next week. She was sure that she had been the intended victim, and had no real fear that he would attack her servant again. Her next thought was to ask Carleton's advice. She wondered a little at this for she was certainly well accustomed to dealing with her own problems, especially since her father had died, but the idea persisted. Perhaps he would know someone who could check on the Comte's movements, without directly involving her.

Lord Carleton meanwhile, had been having his own problems.

He had finally managed to invite Rosamond Lyle out for a drive in his phaeton, and had been looking forward to it. However, once she was actually seated beside him, he found she had little to say apart from commonplaces about the weather. She had no opinions about anything serious and when he did manage to engage her in conversation, it was about the ball she had last attended. Eventually they drew up outside her house and his groom hopped down to hold the horses' heads, while he helped Rosamond to alight. At the same time, Jack Lambert strolled around the corner on his way to call on Amanda and her cousin.

"Hullo there, Richard, and Rosamond, how charming you look this afternoon, your eyes put the sky to shame!" Carleton started to laugh at his friend's exuberance but then he caught sight of Rosamond's blushing face. She was smiling down at Jack, a different person entirely than the one he had been driving around for the past hour. He felt as if he had been punched in the stomach.

So, sits the wind in that quarter he thought wryly, he'd had no inkling. Thank heavens he had not gone so far as to make her an offer, what if she had felt compelled to accept it? He plastered a polite smile on his face, declined an offer to come into the house to pay his respects to Aunt Louisa and said instead that he must see his horses settled.

When Carleton heard his butler answer the door that evening, his first thought was to deny his presence, he felt disinclined for company. But when he heard it was Peter Francis, curiosity changed his mind and he asked the butler to show him into the study.

"Good evening, Peter, what can I do for you? I assume this is not a social call?"

Frances smiled briefly and admitted she had come for his advice. "You said yesterday that I could call on you, I hope you don't mind. When I returned to the inn this evening, I found my servant had been attacked, I think by the Comte Duverne, though I have no proof."

"Your servant?" he queried sharply.

"Yes, in mistake for myself I fancy. The attacker appears to have been waiting in my room and struck John on the head when he came in."

Carleton drew in his breath, disliking the thought that his friend had been in danger. "The Runners? No, perhaps not, as you say there is no evidence," he paused, frowning.

"I wondered if you might be in a position to make enquiries about the Comte for me? But only if it's no trouble," Frances added hastily.

"Yes, I could do that," Carleton answered. He paused for a moment, "I am going out of town tomorrow for a short visit to my estate in Surrey, but I could arrange someone to undertake a discreet investigation into the Comte for us while I am away."

Frances felt her heart drop at the news Carleton was going away.

Before she could say anything, he continued, "As a matter of fact, I've had an idea. Would you like to come with me? The Comte would not be able to bother you there. I have some business to attend to, but I could offer you riding and some shooting while we are there. I intend to be at Chatswood but a week or two - 't would give my agent time to find out what the Comte is about. What do you say? Can you arrange your affairs?" He looked at her.

Frances found herself seriously considering the idea; to be sure there would be risks in staying with Carleton, but they would involve her reputation not her life. She certainly did not want to remain a sitting target at the Pelican for the Comte to waylay at his pleasure.

Taking a deep breath, she nodded, "Thank you, my lord, I accept with pleasure, if you are certain it would not be an inconvenience."

Carleton smiled wryly, "It's not all one sided I assure you, I shall be glad of your company. I leave tomorrow at ten - will that suit you?"

"I'll be here," she promised, a little breathlessly. She left shortly after to make the necessary arrangements, and found that her stomach was churning all the way home with a mixture of fear and excitement.

She made arrangements for John to stay on in his room at the Pelican but cancelled her own as she needed to save the money. Instead she left a small sum in the care of Mrs Cobb to pay the nurse and for any medicines John might require. She took only two bags, and packed both of them to take with her. She wrote a careful note of explanation to John and told the innkeepers she was going into the country for a while to stay with a friend.

Mrs Cobb looked rather taken aback by this show of heartlessness, but could hardly complain considering the arrangements that had been made for John's care. "I suppose 'tis more than some gentlemen would do," she admitted later to her spouse. "A real nurse to look after him an' all." Mr Cobb grunted.

CHAPTER 10

Ten o'clock the next morning, found Frances loading her two bags into the coach Carleton had hired to drive to Surrey. His own four well-matched chestnuts champed impatiently at the bit and his groom clung to the back. As soon as they left the crowded streets of London, Carleton set the horses along at a brisk pace, eager to reach Chatswood by nightfall.

He handled the reins expertly and Frances enjoyed watching him from her seat alongside. At one stage he offered her the reins but she declined, "I've never had much practice, my lord. I'm not sure I could manage them and I am certain I could not keep up this pace."

"So that is one thing I can beat you at, eh?" grinned Carleton. Frances smiled, unruffled, and enjoyed the clean fresh air, breathing deeply. "It is wonderful to get out of London for a few days, everything is so green in England!"

They stopped to change the horses and have a quick bite to eat at an inn, but were soon their way again.

"Chatswood is near a village called Selby," explained Carleton as they drew nearer to their destination. "It has been in my family for about a hundred years, 'tis a snug property, not huge but big enough for my needs. My nearest neighbour is Squire Herbert and his wife. They have a daughter still in the schoolroom and three lads. The youngest may be coming to Chatswood soon to learn the business involved in running an estate with my agent. He is interested in bookkeeping, rather to his father's disgust." He looked at Frances for a minute.

"The squire is a hunting man and cannot see how anyone could be interested in anything else! I shall have to call on him, but there probably will not be time for formal socialising."

Frances nodded, suddenly a little nervous. Just what was she letting herself in for? "I should probably keep a low profile," she offered tactfully. Carleton could scarcely wish to introduce a pro-fessional gamester to his neighbours. London was one thing, but the country was something else entirely.

The sun had just set when they trotted through the gates of Chatswood. The road wound gradually through an avenue of oak trees until it opened suddenly to reveal a circular driveway with a large stone house behind. The building, Frances discovered later, was in the shape of an 'E' with the middle stroke missing and was several stories high. Feeling rather overwhelmed, she got down and followed Carleton up the steps to where an elderly man in black stood waiting to receive him.

"Welcome home, my lord."

"How are you, Williams?" asked his lordship smiling. "This is Mr Francis who will be staying with me for a while." He looked around. "Is Maddy about?"

The butler was smiling too and answered, "Oh yes, my lord, Mrs Madden will be down in a minute."

The groom who had travelled with them, organised the removal of the luggage from the coach and then drove it round the back to the stables. By this time they had been ushered into the hall and a small, neatly dressed woman was almost running down the stairs to greet Carleton. He caught her hands in his and kissed her cheek. "No need to ask how you are, Maddy! As blooming as ever I see!"

She smiled at him, "None of your sauce, my lord," but Frances could tell she was flattered. He let her go and her eyes went to Peter standing behind him. "Peter, this is Mrs Madden, she used to be our governess and now she keeps the house running for me. Maddy, this is Peter Francis, he'll be staying with me." Mrs Madden looked rather closely at Frances, who held her gaze steadily and bowed politely.

She looked suddenly worried, "My lord, you didn't tell me you were bringing a friend. I've only had your room prepared."

"Oh dear," exclaimed his lordship guiltily. "Well perhaps Peter could have a bed made up in my room tonight."

Before Frances could open her mouth to protest, Mrs Madden said hastily and with unexpected firmness, "Nonsense, Mr Richard, that wouldn't do at all. There is the room your cousin had last week on his way up to Yorkshire, that wouldn't take much to make presentable."

"Alright, Maddy, except that Peter can have my room for tonight and I'll have Theo's. Then we won't need to worry about anything until tomorrow. I can tell Peter is nearly asleep on his feet - up all night worrying were you?"

Frances nodded and between conflicting desires not to make any trouble and to collapse as soon as possible, was overrun by Lord Carleton's hospitable instincts. Maddy bowed to the inevitable and disappeared to check on his Lordship's dinner and arrange for clean sheets and a warming pan for his bed.

"I'm very sorry, my lord," apologised Frances, "All this fresh air must have gone to my head. I'm afraid I'm not very good company for you tonight."

"No matter, I'll show you to your room if you like and you can retire immediately."

"Thank you," murmured Frances, stifling a yawn.

The room Carleton had temporarily given up for her was rich and warm looking. Panelled wood covered the walls and a huge four poster bed stood in the centre with crimson curtains drawn back. Thick floral carpet covered the floor, and a large set of drawers opposite matched the cedar panelling. A fire burned cosily in the grate and the window revealed a darkening view of the drive and oak plantations beyond. Carleton drew the gold brocade curtains across the window and went to the door.

"Sleep well, lad. I'll see you at breakfast in the morning?"

Peter nodded and thanked his lordship again for the room. Alone, Frances pulled off her boots and breeches. She took out a masculine looking nightshirt and undressed beneath it on the off chance that a manservant might be sent to assist her. In fact, no sooner had she jumped into bed than someone knocked softly on her door. At her command of 'Enter,' a slight man in servants' livery stepped into the room.

"Lord Carleton asked me to offer my services, sir," he said courteously. "I'm Fanshaw."

"Thank you, Fanshaw. If you would just see to my boots, that would be fine."

"Very good, sir, and perhaps I may take the breeches? I fancy I see a spot of mud on them."

"Oh. Yes, thank you, Fanshaw."

Taking the articles, the manservant bowed noiselessly out of the room. I'll have to be careful around Fanshaw, thought Frances, he'll insist on helping me dress in the morning I'll wager.

She snuggled down under the blankets and was soon sound asleep.

CHAPTER 11

Downstairs, Lord Carleton finished his dinner in solitary state; Mrs Madden, as usual, having refused to join him. Alone, he found himself dwelling on Rosamond's duplicity. Why had she led him on to think she would welcome his attentions if she was in love with someone else? He didn't think now, that he had really loved her but it had been close - he called for a second bottle of claret.

It was a pity Peter had gone to bed, he could have talked him out of the black mood that was pressing down on him. He sat for a long time gazing into the fire and drinking steadily. Eventually he stood up rather carefully and made his way up to bed. The household had retired and quietness lay over everything like a blanket, the light he carried threw vast shadows over the walls.

When he reached his room he looked around for Fanshaw before remembering he had told him not to wait up. Oh well, surely he could manage to take off his own boots for once. He undressed with careful concentration, not that he was by any means drunk by Jove, no, just a little tired. The faint glow from the fire showed the curtains still open around the bed and - he froze. There was a girl's face on the pillow, a girl actually sleeping in his bed!

His mind confused by the claret, he didn't stop to think who it could be or how she had got there. There was only one reason a woman would be in his bed and his first reaction was to throw her out. Before he had even moved however, he had second thoughts. Why not take advantage of what was offered for once? It had been so long since he had slept with a woman. Casting caution to the winds he leant across the bed and kissed the soft lips.

Startled grey eyes opened and the mouth was wrenched away from his. A strong hand thrust him back and a voice cried "No! My lord!" in a shocked, fierce, horrifyingly familiar tone.

In a flash, Carleton was standing back from the bed, his face white with shock. "Oh God! I'm sorry - I didn't - I thought - Oh my God!" he repeated, gathered his clothes up in one arm and fled.

Frances stared after him, her heart thudding like a hammer. What in the name of heaven had he been thinking? He'd looked devastated at her reaction, but how could he seriously believe she would just fall in to his arms? It took a while for her jangled brain to realise Carleton had not been horrified because he thought he had kissed a woman, he thought he had just kissed Peter Francis.

The disaster ran round and round in her mind like a mouse in a cage, trying to find a way out. For a brief moment she considered packing her bags and climbing out the window, but that smacked of bad melodrama. On a more practical note, her boots and breeches were still in the care of Fanshaw, she would have to leave in the morning. Could she pretend she did not remember what had happened? She fell into an uneasy sleep.

Morning came eventually, but no further solution had occurred to her by the time she had packed her bags and made her way down to the breakfast room. To her great relief it was empty. Her stomach was churning, and she helped herself to coffee, unable to face the thought of food. What could she say to him?

Carleton came in. Frances went bright red and could not meet his eyes. "I'm sorry!" she exclaimed, "I'll go straight away."

"I suppose that's the only thing to do," Carleton replied, his voice harsh with strain. He cleared his throat and continued jerkily. "Will you believe me when I say I did not know it was you? I had forgotten we'd changed rooms and when I saw you ... I thought -" he stopped. He could hardly say he'd thought Peter was a girl! "God knows what I thought, but I didn't think it was you, Peter!"

"I know," the words came out in a whisper.

"My God, if I was another type of man I could laugh about this and pretend it was all a jest in poor taste!" He paused again. "You won't - won't speak of this to anyone?"

"Never!" Frances cried, looking at him for the first time. His appearance shocked her. Dark circles under his eyes proved hours of sleepless worry and the tension in every line of his body showed the rigid control he was now exerting on himself. His face was white and drawn, and when she met his eyes she saw agonised shame, and what really shocked her, a touch of fear.

Carleton had not slept for self disgust. It had been a frighteningly short time before the horrifying thought had slid into his mind that perhaps he had known it was Peter, perhaps there was a terrible reason why he had no wife or even a mistress. What would he have done if Peter had kissed him back?

The fear lurking in Carleton's face brought Frances up short, even though she did not fully understand it.

She shook her head decisively, "No, it is not fair! You don't deserve this."

Carlton stared at her, not daring to even imagine what she was leading up to.

"Richard, this will be a shock, but not as great a one as you have had already," she tried to smile and failed. "I must tell you the truth about myself, I have been deceiving you." She took a deep breath. "I am a woman, not a man."

Carleton looked at her in disbelief.

"My name is not really Peter but Frances, with an "e". All that I told you about myself is true, except for that. I disguised myself as a man for my own safety, so I can travel freely and earn my living," she explained carefully, still looking at him. "For most of my life, even when I lived with my father, I was dressed as a boy more often than a girl."

Unconvinced, Carleton shook his head, "I just can't believe it."

"I know it is difficult in these clothes," Frances agreed. "I'll go upstairs and change into a dress, if you will give me ten minutes then come up to my room?"

Carleton looked at her speechlessly, then nodded. As she left the room, he walked over to the window in a daze. What on earth had he let himself in for? Peter (he still thought of him that way) had admitted to him he was an adventurer. Was this some kind of horrible trap to extort money from him? He did not want to believe it, but had everything been an act? No, it was I who kissed him, he reminded himself, still hardly able to bear the thought. Had ten minutes passed yet?

He had to go and see for himself, find out the truth about his sex at least, before he could even start to make any sense of the rest of it.

Frances raced upstairs, thinking only of how she must wipe that terrible look from Richard's face. Her fingers were trembling so much she could barely manage to unlock her bag. Eventually she got it open and scrambled hastily into her green gown. She slipped on the brown wig and dusted a little powder on her face, then stepped into her white slippers as a knock came at the door.

" 'Tis me, Carleton." He wondered fearfully what he would find when Peter opened the door. He heard the key being turned in the lock and then stepped cautiously into the room.

He could scarcely believe his eyes. A young woman stood before him. Peter, no 'Frances' had gently rounded shoulders, unmistakable breasts and a neat waist. Her face looked different too, softer under the curled wig. Needing further reassurance he reached out to touch her. Gently he ran his fingertips down her soft cheek, then down the side of her throat then down to cup her breast with his hand. He could feel it round, heavy and warm through the flimsy material and realised that at least was true, this was definitely a woman! He looked at her again and stepped closer.

Frances had just realised, rather belatedly, that perhaps her bedroom was not the most sensible place she could have chosen to prove she was a woman. She spoke quickly, putting up a hand to hold him off. "I realise this must be very confusing for you, my lord. Will you please leave now, and let me change back to Peter? I will come downstairs and talk to you in a few minutes, I promise."

Carleton stared down at her, grappling with his feelings, uncertain as to whether he wanted to hit her or kiss her, or maybe both!

It was painfully obvious what sort of woman she must be, to live that kind of life.

Made uneasy by his continued silence, Frances spoke again, "Let me go, please." Deliberately, she raised her chin and squared her shoulders like Peter Francis. "The answer is still 'no,' my lord."

Carleton flinched and stepped back. "I have no idea whether I am coming or going," he admitted slowly, "My head is still spinning, I need some time to think."

"Unless you would prefer to be alone, could I suggest we go somewhere else to talk? Riding, perhaps?"

"That sounds the safest idea under the circumstances. I'll send word to the stables." He turned on his heel and walked out quickly, shutting the door firmly behind him. He leant against it for a second, fighting a mad desire to rush back in and - too late. He heard the key turn in the lock. It was probably for the best, he was scarcely thinking clearly at the moment. Her voice came to him through the door as if she knew he was still there. "Just don't forget I'm a man, my lord. For Heaven's sake do not order me a side saddle!"

CHAPTER 12

Half an hour later, two horses were saddled and waiting down in front of the stables and Carleton was growing anxious. She was coming, wasn't she? Or had the suggestion been a ruse so she could quietly leave? The thought that she might have gone was like a blow to the stomach. As he was about to send someone to find out, Frances came hurrying into the yard. She was dressed as Peter Francis in rather faded but clean riding breeches and boots, her stride long and crisp.

"My apologies for keeping you waiting, my lord, I overslept," she cried gaily. "Oh what beautiful animals! Which one may I ride?" The groomsman led forward a beautiful roan gelding with a proud head and liquid amber eyes. They all talked horses for a while, though Frances admitted freely she did not know as much as the other two men.

Carleton had a big black stallion which was snorting impatiently to be off. "Right my beauty? Let's go then." The black danced for a minute as he got him under control and they trotted out of the yard at a brisk pace. Frances rode well, if not superbly, but he found he couldn't take his eyes off her. Now that he knew she was a woman he wondered how he could have been so blind before.

While they had been in the stable yard he had been in an agony of trepidation that the groom would recognise her for what she was. Certainly the flattened chest and squared shoulders were a powerful aid, but it was also the way she moved and the care she took with her mannerisms. People saw what they expected to see.

He felt as if his head was split in two. Half of it saw the young man whose company he enjoyed and whose skills he admired and the other half saw a young woman with smooth skin, an enchanting smile and beautiful eyes. He realised that those same eyes were smiling quizzically at him now. "Shall we gallop?" she called.

For answer he dug his heels into Diablo's sides and they flew off, hooves pounding on the turf. Frances followed on her roan but they could not match the pace of the other two and soon fell behind. His lordship obviously knew his grounds better than she did, and she was content to follow, enjoying the speed and feel of powerful muscles beneath her. Eventually the pair ahead drew up and she brought her horse to a stop beside them.

"That was wonderful," she cried breathlessly. They moved on at a walking pace to cool the horses. For a moment neither spoke, each busy with their own thoughts. Frances broke the silence, her eyes straight ahead.

"Before I go, I owe you an explanation. What I tell you will be the truth, but of course it is up to you to decide if you believe me or not." She looked at him then, but he merely nodded for her to continue. "As I told you, my name is Frances, but I know of no other. My father indeed had so many names over the years I could scarce keep track of them. I think he was of gentle birth for he always knew how to go on in polite company and I know he went to school here at Eton, but there was no money and we always lived off the cards." She paused to reach forward and pat her horse's neck.

"My mother died when I was a small child and even before that I think we moved around a lot. Often it was easier for me to be a boy, for my own protection as much as anything, and I learned how to shoot and fence and ride, but I don't have many feminine accomplishments - apart from French and Italian of course. Do not misunderstand me, it was a wonderful life and I have no regrets," she added with a touch of defiance. Carleton looked as if he would protest this, but he thought better of it and motioned for her to continue.

"As I told you, my father died a few months ago and it was at his request that I came to London, to follow up a name he had given me, someone who might be of assistance to me. I had planned to lay low until I could find this person, I did not intend to get caught up in your affairs at all, my lord, but then I did and I must admit it was very exciting," she smiled tentatively at him.

"And then, as you know, the Comte Duverne struck down my servant and is hot after my blood so I took refuge here with you, intending to do no more than be a companion to you as Peter Francis until I could plan my next move." She shrugged her shoulders, "The best laid plans eh? I will not trouble you any further, I will go as soon as we get back to the house."

Carleton surprised both of them then by leaning forward to catch the roan's bridle.

"I will not let you go," he said, rather fiercely. Both horses had stopped and he kept his grip on the reins so that their legs were nearly touching.

Frances looked at him levelly. "What do you mean, my lord? Whatever you may think of my behaviour, I am not a whore." He flinched at this and she continued. "'Tis true I am a gamester and an adventuress if you like, but I have been no man's mistress, ever!" A spot of scarlet burned in each cheek as she said this. "I know the world would say I might as well be for coming here with you unchaperoned, but most people would have damned me long ago for the life I have led. But they would be wrong!"

Carleton felt more than a little shocked by this plain speaking, especially when he realised he had been thinking those very things himself.

"My lord, I am very sorry for the distress I have caused you, but I ask you to remember that you were friends with Peter and to let me go." Frances said quietly, not making any effort to free herself.

Carleton looked searchingly at her, "I must confess my head is still at sixes and sevens over all this." He sighed and released his hold on her horse. "I will not force you to anything, but - I do not want you to return to London alone to be hunted by Duverne."

"You do not need to be concerned, sir, I will manage," she murmured.

Carleton was still considering, a frown between his eyes. For the first time in his life he was contemplating taking a mistress, but only an idiot would have made such a suggestion now. "What if you stayed here for a few more days? As Peter Francis. Do you think we could keep up the masquerade a little longer?"

Frances was amazed. "Pardon?"

"Could we return to our previous relationship, pretend last night never occurred? I have some business here I must complete, before I return to London. I give you my word you would be safe here."

"Lord Carleton, are you certain of this? You would be prepared to have me stay here as Peter Francis, knowing what you do about me?" Frances felt bewildered, she had been certain he would never forgive her for the deception.

Her companion was not actually certain about anything at the moment, except that he did not want her to go. This was the only way he could think of to persuade her and to give himself some breathing space. "My word on it."

"Thank you! I did not expect ... I did not think you ..."Frances struggled to express her feelings, she felt close to tears. "You are too kind. I will accept your offer, but only on the condition that you tell me to leave if my presence becomes ... inconvenient."

"Agreed. Perhaps we should return?" They cantered side by side back to the stables.

CHAPTER 13

Frances went upstairs to change and found that a new room had been prepared for her, a few doors down from Carleton's. She still had a view of the front drive but it was decorated in blue and cream without the rich wood panelling. Her clothes had been unpacked and put away, with the exception of course of those in her locked bag. A basin of warm water had been provided and she washed up before going downstairs, feeling hungry after her ride. A cold luncheon was laid out on the sideboard and she helped herself to a large plate of cold meat while she waited for his lordship. He joined her shortly and they sat down at the table.

"I intend to call on the Squire this afternoon," he advised. "Will you be alright here?"

"Yes indeed. I will practice my shooting if that is acceptable," Frances replied, relieved that he had not asked her to go with him. She needed some time alone. Although she knew she could trust Carleton, he had given her his word, she was anxious about whether his scheme would work. She had noticed he was already treating her differently than he had Peter Francis.

When they returned from their ride, he had stepped towards her as if he would assist her to dismount, a courtesy he would have offered without thinking to any woman of his acquaintance. Hastily she had swung out of the saddle protesting, "No - no, I can manage thank you. I am quite recovered!"

Carleton had come to an abrupt halt, realising his mistake. "Of course. I'm sorry, Peter."

Meanwhile Carleton was being welcomed by Squire Herbert and his wife. Part of him was conducting a civil conversation but another part was still thinking about Frances. He had yet to recover from the shock that she was a woman. Immense relief had been his initial reaction because it had released him from a private hell, but then he had felt furiously angry that he had made such a fool of himself.

Now however, his feelings were more complicated, and sheer amazement was not the least of them. How incredible that she should have fenced so well with Maestro Mancini and outshot his friends and himself so brilliantly.

"While you are here, Richard," the Squire was saying, "I was wondering if I might send Jeremy over to you, to meet your agent and see what the work would entail. Give him a chance to decide if that is what he wants to do with his life."

Carleton nodded his agreement. Jeremy was the son who was interested in learning about estate management. Squire Herbert filled him in on the local news until eventually he took his leave and swung himself onto Diabolo to complete his appointed round of visits.

Back at Chatswood, Frances finished her shooting practice and returned to the house. The thought had occurred to her that she might find some reference to the Murray family in one of the many books in the library. Mrs Madden showed her into the room pleasantly enough, but she fancied that for some reason the housekeeper disapproved of her. At one time she caught a speculative look in her eyes and wondered for a moment if by any chance she had guessed she was not what she seemed.

"She is probably merely anxious to see that I am not imposing myself on Carleton," Frances concluded reassuringly. "Which of course, I am!" she admitted with a wry smile. There was a comfortable deep leather armchair in the library and she curled up cosily in it with a pile of books at her elbow. Carleton found her there on his return. Frances immediately stretched her legs out in a more masculine pose, then sat forward, her arms on her knees.

"Hullo, what are you reading?"

Frances smiled up at him, "I am looking through some local histories." She paused and said consideringly, "You may be able to help me more though. Do you know anything about a Lady Julia Murray?"

He frowned, "Murray? No I don't think so... wait a minute, I believe there is an older lady of that name living in London, but I think her Christian name is Anna. Would she be the one? It is coming back to me now ... I remember there was a daughter, or perhaps two, but I am fairly sure she died some years ago. Maddy might know more, shall I ask her?"

A disappointed expression came over Frances face as he spoke and she chewed her lip. "I do wish he had told me more!" she murmured to herself.

Carleton looked at her inquiringly.

"I am sorry, my lord, it is merely that my father told me to seek out Lady Julia Murray when I reached London, but I have no idea who she is or what he expected to come of it! It is very puzzling."

Carleton pulled up another chair and asked her to tell him her father's exact words. She did so and he agreed that it was certainly not much to go on. "Perhaps she is some sort of relation?" he queried. "That would seem to be the most likely reason he would ask you to find her."

"I hardly think so, after all my father never mentioned her before then. As I told you, I don't know which of the names he used was his own, if any, but I am sure he never used Murray." She answered doubtfully.

"What was your mother's maiden name, do you know?" pursued Carleton.

"Emerson I think."

He frowned, "That is not familiar to me either. Shall I ask Maddy to join us?"

"Yes, if she would."

Carleton went off to find her and returned in a few minutes, Mrs Madden puffing slightly at his heels. "Have a seat, Maddy, I would like to ask you something. A glass of sherry?"

The housekeeper was soon settled comfortably on a chair in front of the fire and Carleton asked "I was wondering if you knew anything about a Lady Julia Murray or her family?"

"Julia Murray?" repeated the housekeeper, narrowing her eyes in concentration. "Let me see. She married Sir Thomas Pointon, rather late in life I believe, but she died in that boating accident in the Channel about three or four years ago now. She had a younger sister I remember, there was some sort of scandal connected with her a long time ago - I fancy she died abroad somewhere. There is only the mother left now to my knowledge, Lady Anna. What is your interest in the family, my lord?"

"Not me, 'tis Peter," he explained. "It appears he has some connection with the family but we are not sure exactly what."

Maddy raised her eyebrows and looked at her doubtfully.

"Thank you for your help, Mrs Madden, perhaps I will call on Lady Murray when I return to London," said Frances, not wanting to tell her the whole story.

"Yes, and I can make some enquiries for you as well," agreed Carleton.

At that point, the footman arrived to announce that dinner was ready. Both of them did full justice to the dishes prepared for them. The food was plentiful but fairly plain, his lordship not having gone to the trouble of bringing his French chef with him from London. Frances entertained him with some stories from her life in Florence and he returned with some of the livelier anecdotes circulating the London drawing rooms.

They opened a second bottle of claret between them and enjoyed themselves thoroughly. If sometimes the glances Carleton bestowed on his companion were a little warmer than those to be expected for such a recent acquaintance, he was not aware of it, and the footman put it down to him being a little merry, not foxed exactly but certainly on the go. Eventually, the remains were cleared away and the port brought out.

"Shall we play cards tonight?" invited Carleton, sitting back in his chair.

"By all means, as long as we play no more than a penny a point," answered Frances.

They took their glasses into the study where there was a warm fire burning merrily in the grate, and Carleton passed a pack of unopened cards across to Frances. She shuffled them professionally. "Whist, sir?"

Carleton nodded. They both played cautiously at first, taking each other's measure. The luck ran with Carleton at first, but even so Frances could see that he was a skilful player. "I would need to keep a clear head if ever we should have a serious game, my lord!"

He laughed and continued to win points, "Would you like another drink? Some brandy perhaps?"

"No thank you, I have had quite enough! Could I have some coffee instead?"

"That's a good idea, I could do with some myself."

By the time the footman had brought the coffee and it had been drunk, Carleton had won five shillings and Frances conceded him the winner.

"If you do not mind, my lord, I will retire for the night. It has been a long day," she added.

"Yes indeed, I feel as if I had been burning the candle at both ends myself." Carleton followed her upstairs and paused at her door.

"Good night, Frances," he said unthinkingly as he opened the door for her.

"Do not call me that, my lord, whatever you do," she whispered urgently. "Someone may overhear you and we will both be in the suds! Just think of me as Peter, nothing else."

Carleton looked at her, seeing her as 'male' again and felt suddenly uncomfortable. Not only was he beginning to grow accustomed to her short curls and breeches, but if truth be told he found them very attractive.

"You are right! I will see you tomorrow, then," He nodded curtly and moved swiftly to his own room.

Three more days passed, filled with riding, long walks and interspersed with meals and conversation. They played cards in the evening for small sums and laughed a lot. Frances continued to practice her shooting when Carleton was involved in the business of the estate and also to delve into the local history books which she found fascinating. Occasionally she found Mrs Madden studying her with a curious eye and she would make an extra effort to do something boyish such as cracking a walnut in her hand or skinning the rabbit she had shot.

Meanwhile Squire Herbert was wrestling with a dilemma. Such a shocking thing had occurred that he would not have believed it if he had not seen it with his own eyes. He was very worried. He valued his own standing in the neighbourhood as a respectable man, who others could look up to as an example, but he was also old fashioned, with a deeply inbred awe of those he considered his betters. The two qualities warred within him until he reached a reluctant decision. He would seek a meeting with Lord Carleton the very next morning.

CHAPTER 14

Carleton was just finishing a rather late breakfast with Peter when the message was brought to him that the Squire was wishful of speaking to him urgently on a serious matter.

"I had better see him now," he apologised to his companion, with whom he had been about to engage in a fencing match when they finished eating.

"Of course, go ahead, I am nearly done here." Frances drained her coffee cup.

Carleton sent back a message for the Squire to await him in the study and soon joined him after brushing the crumbs from his waistcoat and straightening his cravat.

"Yes, Squire?" he asked, pulling the door closed behind him but failing to notice that it had not latched. "What's the problem?"

Squire Herbert did not return his smile but continued to look very solemn.

Clearing his throat, he replied, "I've come to tell you, my Lord, that I won't be sending young Jeremy over here. I've changed my mind."

"Oh?" queried Carleton in surprise. "Doesn't he want to be an agent anymore?"

"Well yes, but I thought I would send him up to Oxford for a year or so first, give him a wider experience."

"But I thought one of the main reasons for him to stay here and learn from Martin was because his health was not good enough to risk college life!" protested the other man, puzzled.

Squire Herbert looked somewhat flurried but repeated doggedly. "It will do him good, a year at Oxford. Make a man of him, after all, he is young yet to be choosing a career."

Carleton considered him frowningly. Something was not right here. Will Herbert, whom he had known for years as a blunt man, had not quite met his eyes once, almost as if he had offended him in some way.

In a different tone, he said, "Come on, Will, stop pitching me a Banbury story! What is the real trouble? Why don't you want Jeremy to come here?"

The Squire reddened then burst out uncomfortably, "I saw you, my Lord, yesterday in Hough's Wood. I can't let the boy come here!"

Neither man noticed the door had opened slightly further behind them.

For a minute Carleton stared uncomprehendingly at him. Then he remembered, he had been walking in the wood with Frances. They had left their horses tied to a tree on the edge and gone for a walk down a narrow winding path, bordered with occasional clumps of bluebells, to where he had promised to show her a large patch of blackberries ready for picking. Hastily he searched his memory, what on earth had he done? Nothing that he could think of. The Squire must have been walking through the wood, taking the shortcut to the village but what the deuce had he seen?

Frances had been delighted with the ripe luscious blackberries and he had helped her pick a basketful to take back. True, he had carried the basket for her but that was unexceptional surely? They had laughed a good deal and he had helped untangle her from the brambles yes - but nothing to cause a scandal there ... Well, certainly not for a man and a woman, but ... for two men? Perhaps not! It was scarcely the done thing for one man to help another out of a patch of briars, and laughingly wipe away the blackberry juice around his mouth with a handkerchief.

And so the Squire did not want to send young Jeremy to him to be corrupted. A furious protest rushed to his lips to die a strangled death as he realised he could not betray Frances. Feeling sick he answered unconvincingly, "'Tis not what it appeared, Will, I promise you!"

When she had heard the Squire's anguished accusation from the study, Frances had known instantly what the problem was, if not the precise cause of it. She spent a frozen minute wondering what to do - there was no time to dash upstairs and throw on a dress. All she could do was to take out the shoulder padding from her jacket and loosen the binding over her breasts. She stepped quickly into the nearby library, no one would be in there this time of day and tore off her jacket and shirt to make the necessary adjustments. Working as fast as she could she rebuttonned the shirt but let the jacket hang open. In a minute she was back at the study door, pasting a saucy smile on her face and pushing it open.

She saw two startled faces turn towards her, one red and horribly uncomfortable and the other white and sick.

"Frances!" Carleton started involuntarily towards her.

"Oh pardon, mon seigneur," she exclaimed in French, "Je m'excuse!"

The Squire stared at the young man who had entered the room. Frances put a hand to her mouth, looked from one to the other and gave a little giggle of embarrassment. The Squire looked harder and turned to glare at Carleton. "What rig are you trying to run here? That's no boy!" The exclamation burst out of him.

Carleton was still staring at her rather blankly, then turned to the Squire and said, "Forgive me, I haven't introduced you. Squire Herbert, this is Frances my - er - "

"Amie," said Frances at the same moment Carleton said, "Betrothed". They stared at each other.

Afterwards the Squire was certain his jaw had dropped a foot, why on earth hadn't Carleton told him the truth instead of letting him say what he had? The shocked astonishment on Frances' face however explained a good deal to him. If she was his betrothed, he was a Bond Street Beau. Nevertheless it appeared Carleton was going to do the right thing and marry her, for after that public declaration he could be sued for breach of promise.

He bowed, "Pleased to meet you, m'selle. May I ask when the wedding is to be?" He felt a spurt of satisfaction at the start this gave both of them, after all he had been made to look a bit of a fool this morning. He looked sideways at Carleton. "Doing it too brown, my lord! I'll bid you good day then."

He picked up his stick and showed himself out.

Frances had been totally astounded when Carleton called her his betrothed. For one delirious second she thought he meant it, and then reality crashed in and she realised the declaration for what it was, a chivalrous impulse uttered on the spur of the moment to protect her. How he was going to explain it later to Squire Herbert was obviously not something he had yet thought of.

She managed a small smile, "Well, I think we brushed through that tolerably well!"

"Frances!" Carleton stretched a hand towards her.

Suddenly she didn't want to hear him explaining to her, or much worse, pretending that he had meant it.

She broke in, "Thank you, Richard, that was a kind thought but it was not really necessary. After all, the Squire will never see me again." She started edging towards the door. "I must go upstairs and straighten up."

CHAPTER 15

Carleton had surprised himself as well as Frances when he had called her his betrothed. His thoughts and feelings were still in turmoil, but when he had seen her gaily confronting the Squire he had not wanted her treated with any less respect than she deserved. As soon as the word was out, he realised how right it sounded. All vague lingering thoughts about Rosamond withered on the spot. How could he ever have imagined spending more than a few hours with her?

Frances had burst into his life, shocking him, entertaining him and oversetting every notion he had ever had of a well brought up young lady and now he wanted her. He reached out again to her but she drew back awkwardly rushing into hasty speech, her eyes not meeting his.

"Frances!" he repeated. "It is alright, I won't embarrass you with a declaration now. But the sooner you return to being a woman, and I can call on you properly, the better. It may be easier for you to be a man but it's been downright disastrous for me!" He laughed.

She smiled woodenly and murmured, "We will see. I must go to my room for a moment, my lord."

"I will see you at dinner then," he announced with a smile. "I have to ride over to Selby this afternoon to finalise some business matters, we will talk more when I return."

Frances escaped to the safety of her room and stood staring blindly out the window. What a disaster! She had achieved the last thing she had ever intended, to trick Richard into making an offer for her. Who would believe it had not been her intention all along? How could she have served him such a turn? She was suddenly furious with herself, she should have left as soon as Richard knew she was a woman, instead of indulging herself by staying on, pretending to be his friend, while falling further in love with him every day.

Yes, she admitted to herself, she had fallen head over heels in love with him. How could she not? And now she had been offered what she longed for most in the world but could not take it, she would have to leave and never see him again.

Tears were trickling down her cheeks as she packed her bags again. She could not stay a moment longer. I cannot face him again, thought Frances, I will have to leave now, while he is away in Selby. I'll borrow the roan and ride to Guildford, then I can leave the horse at the inn and take the stage from there.

She would have to leave a letter. What reason could she give for her abrupt departure? She tore up three attempts before she managed a brief note which said simply,

"My lord,

Forgive me but I cannot stay any longer. It is time for the masquerade to end. Please do not try to find me.

I wish you well,

F"

She folded it twice, wrote his name on it and left it propped on the mantelpiece of her room. Then it was time to leave.

Picking up her two heavy bags, she realised for the first time that it might not be quite so simple to walk out of the house and leave with her luggage while her host was absent. If a servant challenged her, what could she say?

As if her very thoughts had conjured her up, Mrs Madden appeared at the top of the stairs, her face a picture of virtuous disapproval. She stared at Frances, taking in the travelling cloak and the two bags, "I heard you in the study. You'll be leaving him then?"

Frances stared back. "'Tis for the best," was all she could think to say.

"You should never have come at all!" the housekeeper stated fiercely, "But I will help you leave. How were you planning to get away?"

"I thought to borrow the roan, and leave it at the inn at Guildford," she replied, startled into telling the truth.

Mrs Madden thought quickly. "I said I will help you - give the bags to me and I will arrange for them to be carried to the front gate. You can pick them up from there. Then it will look as if you are just going for a ride. Well? The sooner you are gone the better!"

"Here they are. I cannot thank you enough!"

"I am not doing it for you!" she interrupted, taking the bags. "I will put them in a basket and get the kitchen boy to take it down to the gatehouse, he won't need to know what is inside."

Without another word, the housekeeper turned and went downstairs, carrying Frances' possessions.

Frances swallowed silently and followed her down to the hall, then went out the door to the stables. It seemed to take forever until the groom had the roan saddled, "It is a grand day for a ride," he commented cheerfully.

Frances agreed, then mounted up and walked her horse slowly down the drive to the gate, keeping an anxious eye out for anyone else around. Where was the basket? Had the housekeeper changed her mind? No, there it was! Quickly she dismounted and it was the work of a moment to tie the bags onto the saddle and climb back up. She took a last look back towards the house then trotted off in the direction of Guildford, with any luck it would be several hours before Richard returned and discovered her flight.

Twelve miles later, she reached Guildford and soon found the inn. It was bustling with horses and carriages, much more than usual surely? "What has been happening here?" she asked an ostler, as she made arrangements for the roan to be stabled until Lord Carleton was able to send his groom for him.

"It's the fight, sir. There was a mill between Gentleman Joe and the Guildford champion. Did you miss it then?"

"I am afraid so," confessed Frances. "Can you tell me when the stage to London is due?"

"Well you've missed the one today, sir. The next is not 'til tomorrow at midday."

Before she could decide what to do, she heard her name.

"Francis? Is that you?" called a familiar voice. Frances looked up and saw Jack Lambert and Harry Belmont coming across the yard towards her. She walked towards them, moving quickly out of the ostler's hearing.

"Great turn up wasn't it? No mere flourishing." cried Harry, beaming with enthusiasm.

"I feel a fool but I missed the whole show! I arrived just as it finished!" she complained, laughing. "I was staying with a friend at Bristow and he dropped me off but we got the time wrong between us and now I hear the stage is not due until tomorrow!"

"Come with us," offered Lambert. "We've got room haven't we, Harry?"

"Are you sure?" asked Frances, picking up her baggage. In no time at all she was seated in the post chaise, barrelling along the road to London, encouraging her companions to talk about the mill they had just witnessed so that they did not think to ask her too many questions about her own activities.

CHAPTER 16

Lord Carleton returned from his trip to Selby feeling tired and looking forward to his dinner. He was also thinking about Frances. They would play cards again and then, now they were betrothed, he would kiss her. He had been celibate so long that now he could hardly wait. There was no need for a long engagement surely, the thought that Frances would refuse his offer never even entered his head.

He knew the way of things and a young woman in Frances' position would not be so foolish as to refuse an offer of marriage, especially from a man as beforehand with the world as himself. His mind was racing ahead, perhaps she would let him take her in his arms, and he would hold her tightly against him, then run his hands over ... he felt hot just imagining it.

He had his first inkling that all was not well when he rode Diabolo around to the stables.

"Did Mr Francis not find you then?" asked his groom looking a little worried. "He has not returned so I thought he must have caught up with you."

"No, I saw no-one. We must have missed each other," replied Carleton, "Tell me what happened again, Toby."

"He took the roan out for a ride, not long after you left, my lord. He said he would take the road to Selby and might try and meet up with you."

"How long ago?"

"Must be all of three hours now," said the groom.

"Peter is a careful rider, 'tis probably too soon to think of accidents. 'Tis only just starting to get dark now," Carleton thought aloud. "I am sure he will return soon."

He left the stables and went into the house, only slightly anxious.

"Hold dinner until Peter returns, if you would," he told Mrs Madden who had come forward to let him know dinner would be ready in half an hour, to allow him time to change his clothes.

She gave him an odd look, then said flatly, "There is no use waiting my lord, your friend has gone."

"What!" exclaimed Carleton.

"Urgent business in town, my lord," she improvised.

"Nonsense!" Carleton rushed up the stairs to Frances' room. No, he could not believe it. All her things were gone. He stood staring, his brain grappling with the shock. Then he saw the letter on the mantelpiece and strode forward to snatch it up.

"My lord,

Forgive me but I cannot stay any longer. It is time for the masquerade to end. Please do not try to find me.

I wish you well,

F"

What did she mean? Had she not understood he was intending to honour the betrothal? He had been so certain she enjoyed his company and was even coming to feel affection for him. How could she leave him like this?

He turned back to the housekeeper who was watching him silently from the doorway.

"What did he say? Where did he go? Tell me everything!" he demanded.

Mrs Madden pursed her lips in disapproval. "There's no need to continue this charade, my lord. I know the truth. All she told me, was that she had urgent business to attend to in London. She said she would ride to Guildford and leave the horse there for you, then take the stage." Mrs Madden tried not to sound defensive.

"Something must have happened! Did anyone come to the house?" He was so worried about Frances, that the knowledge that Mrs Madden knew her secret scarcely made an impact.

'No, my lord," Mrs Madden stuck to the simple story. She had not thought to invent a tale and probably would have been unable to carry it off successfully if she had.

"She must still be in Guildford, the stage would have already departed by the time she would have reached the inn," Carleton was thinking aloud. "I will have to go after her and bring her back."

"No! Let her go, master Richard," the words were torn out of her. "A woman like that! Think of your reputation, your family!"

"'Tis not your affair, Maddy, stay out of it!" Carleton retorted angrily. He strode though the house to the door. "I don't know when I'll be back, expect me when you see me!" he flung over his shoulder.

Diabolo was soon saddled again and Carleton was off to Guildford as fast as he could ride while there was still enough light to
see by. The moon would be up later but he would have to slow
down until then, a fall from his horse would help no-one.

An hour later, he rode up to the King's Head and was met by
the innkeeper himself, smoothing down his apron and looking
questioningly at him.

"My Lord Carleton, is anything the matter? What can I do for
you?"

Carleton dismounted and handed the reins to a hovering stable
boy, "Just walk him up and down for me will you?" he told him then
turned to the innkeeper.

"Evening, Jackson. My business is with a young man I think you
have staying here, Peter Francis. Could you take me up to him?"

But the innkeeper was shaking his head, "Got no-one of that
name, no young gentleman staying here at all, your lordship."

"He brought my horse in this afternoon, the roan," persisted
Carleton.

"Oh him! No, he's long gone, he went off with Mr Lambert in his
chaise, here for the fight he was. We have your horse though, all
right and tight in the stable. No trouble is there, my lord?" the
innkeeper added, suddenly anxious. His lordship had an awfully
queer look in his eyes.

Carleton felt as if he had been kicked in the stomach. Jack
Lambert, again. First Rosamond and now Frances preferred him.
He couldn't believe it. Was he so repulsive? Jack so attractive?

He realised the innkeeper was still waiting for his answer and
managed to say casually, "No, no trouble, I just hoped to catch him
before he left. No matter. I'll ride the roan back now I am here, if

you could bring him out? I'll lead Diablo." He gave the innkeeper a generous sum to make up for the inconvenience, refused a glass of wine and was on his way home in a matter of minutes.

What was she thinking? He asked himself. Jack certainly will not offer marriage to her. Does she prefer to be his mistress rather than my wife? He felt sick. His thoughts went round and round in his head as he rode. He felt angry, hurt and offended all at once. But I am not thinking straight, he suddenly realised, as far as Jack is concerned she is a man, Frances has merely accepted a ride from him, that is all. It is still true that she has run away rather than marry me but at least she hasn't run to someone else!

He considered returning to London the next day to find her and demand to know what was happening, but when he woke in the morning after an overcooked dinner and a poor night's sleep, he decided it would be more sensible to stay and finish the business he had arranged and depart in two days time as scheduled. He decided that he needed a period of sober reflection before dashing off in pursuit of her. Perhaps when he saw her again he would offer a carte blanche instead of marriage, he thought, in a fit of pique.

Chapter 17

Eventually the three travellers in the post chaise reached London and dropped a weary Frances in front of the Pelican. She was greeted by a relieved Mrs Cobb.

"I am that glad to see you again, sir, and that's the truth! You would not believe the trouble we've had getting that man of yours to stay in bed. As soon as my back was turned, up he'd get, determined to be off after you. I don't know how many times I told him you'd be safe enough with his lordship." She shook her head, following Frances up to the room.

"Nurse would have it he was delirious. In the end she put a stop to it by taking away his clothes."

"Oh dear," said Frances guiltily, "Perhaps now that I am here you could bring them back. I am sorry for all your trouble. Could I have a room for the night?"

"Of course, sir, I'll see to it at once."

"If John is well enough, we will be on our way tomorrow. I am due to visit my cousin in Bath," announced Frances.

One look at the scowling invalid's face convinced Frances there was nothing that a good raking down of herself would not cure, and in a few minutes the nurse was politely but firmly dismissed with a final payment for her services, along with Mrs Cobb, and Frances leant against the wall letting the tirade wash over her. The manservant had been vastly worried to learn, when he eventually came to his senses, that his mistress had gone off into the country with Lord Carleton. Eventually her servant ran out of steam and lay glaring at her.

Frances smiled, "I am glad you are so much better, John! Do you think you will be fit to leave tomorrow?"

"Another minute would not be soon enough!" he growled. "Pesky women! What devilry are you up to now?"

"No devilry at all! Why just the opposite! I intend to establish a respectable residence at the Regent Hotel – it is time for me to meet Lady Murray. I have been thinking that, whatever the connection I have with the family, they will be bound to make enquiries and a respectable hotel is the best background I can think of. I shall say I have just come over from France and have no acquaintance here in London that I could stay with. I have enough money to pay for a fortnight's accommodation, which should be quite sufficient because by then I will either have been invited to stay with Lady Murray or I will have to be off adventuring again!"

John nodded with grudging approval, "You will need the devil's own luck to pull clear out of this one though, Miss Frances!"

The next day she paid her shot at the inn and sent her servant on ahead to book rooms at the Regent. Dressed neatly as a respectable young matron, Frances visited several employment agencies and was lucky enough to engage a middle aged French woman who spoke hardly any English, having come to England with her émigré mistress but then been cast off as being too expensive a luxury. Frances bound her to secrecy by promising her the price of the fare back to Paris once the two weeks were over.

That very afternoon, Miss Frances White and her companion Madame Lebrun moved quietly into their modest suite of rooms at the Regent.

Twenty four hours later, Frances found herself alighting from a hackney coach, with her new companion behind her and treading up the steps towards a blue door with a brass knocker in the centre. She wore her yellow morning dress which was clean and tidy, if not exactly fashionable and had tied a modest bonnet over her hair. Feeling nervous despite herself she knocked firmly at the door. It was opened by a footman, dressed in a shade of blue which matched the colour of the door.

"Is Lady Murray at home, please?" she asked in a clear, low voice.

"Who may I say is calling, Miss?" he asked dubiously.

"Please tell her that Henry Metcalf sent me," answered Frances taking the bull by the horns.

The footman stared curiously and asked her to wait, then disappeared, shutting the door behind him. Frances considered again, the reasons she had come. Foremost was curiosity. She had learnt all she could from common gossip and it had not been much. She still could not imagine what connection the Murrays had with her father, nor was she really sure that the lady she hoped to see today was the one he had directed her to. Still, it was all she had to go on, she certainly would not find out anything more waiting in her room at the Regent.

Just as she was wondering if she had been forgotten, the foot-man returned and ushered her inside.

"Lady Murray will see you, Miss," he sounded surprised, even to himself. "If you will just come this way to the morning salon. Your companion can wait here." She followed him upstairs and along a passage. Frances was concentrating on the approaching interview and scarcely noticed the magnificent surroundings. The footman pushed open a door in front of her and announced, "The young, er lady, my Lady."

Frances stepped into the room. For some reason she had been expecting an invalid, perhaps because everyone had spoken of her as a recluse, but the woman standing before her looked as fit and sharp as a tack. She wore a fashionable dark grey gown and her thick white hair was coiled on top of her head. Bright blue eyes stared at her with strange intensity and she noticed the fingers of her right hand were clenched whitely around a French fan.

"Well?" the query was more command than question. "What message do you have for me from that man? Speak up, girl. His name had not been spoken in this house for over twenty five years until today – I want to know what he wants after all this time."

It was not an auspicious opening. Obviously the unknown Mr Metcalf had seriously incurred her Ladyship's wrath and was not a passport to her goodwill as her father had hoped. Feeling her cause lost already, Frances felt she had nothing to lose and answered honestly.

"I am sorry for intruding on you, my lady, but I was advised to come to London and seek out a Lady Julia Murray and to mention Henry Metcalf. Unfortunately I hear she has passed away and so

I have come to see you instead ..." She broke off as the woman in front of her seemed to sway suddenly.

"Tom, a chair!" she called imperiously. The footman hastily pulled forward a gilt chair and bent over her, making sure she was settled comfortably. "Nothing to worry about, don't fuss, Tom." She complained. "What's your name, girl?"

"Frances, my lady."

"Frances Metcalf, eh?" she queried with a sardonic curl to her lip.

"If I am, it is the first I have heard of it! As far as I know, Henry Metcalf was not my father," she replied coolly.

"What in heavens' name do you mean, girl? Who are you then?" Lady Murray frowned crossly.

"Perhaps you could answer a question for me first, my lady. Can you please tell me who Henry Metcalf is?"

CHAPTER 18

The question fell like a pebble in a pond, sending out waves of bewildered silence. The old lady drew in her breath then spoke slowly, "I do not understand, I quite thought ... when I heard ... I think you should tell me the full story of how you came to be here."

"Very well, my lady. I must explain a little of my history first."

"In that case," Lady Murray interrupted, "Tom, would you please ask Mrs Pearson to come down here? I would like her to hear this." She turned to Frances as Tom went to the door and sent another servant on the errand. "Mrs Pearson is my companion," she explained briefly, "She was my children's nurse – I hope she will be able to help me prove if you are who you claim to be or not."

"As I have not claimed to be anybody at all, I rather think she will have trouble with that!" retorted Frances acidly. This brought a brief smile to the other woman's face for the first time.

In a few moments the footman returned with a plump elderly woman leaning on his arm, her black eyes snapping with curiosity.

"Yes, my lady? What did – Oh!" she broke off as she caught sight of Frances. "Oh I am sorry, I did not know you had ..." for a second time she broke off what she was saying.

"Well?" queried Lady Murray impatiently.

Mrs Pearson stared at Frances, her head tilted to one side, struggling with the resemblance. "Would you mind taking off your bonnet Miss, so that I can see your face more clearly?"

Curious, Frances complied, revealing the new blond, curled wig which most resembled the natural colour of her hair.

"Master Henry!" gasped the woman clutching her throat. Frances shot a quick look at Lady Murray and saw a quick flash of disappointment. "Henry?" she questioned.

Mrs Pearson kept her eyes on the young woman before her. "Henry," she repeated firmly, "although her eyes are gray, not brown, the resemblance is striking."

"Would somebody please tell me who the deuce is Henry?" demanded Frances in a loud voice.

"Why your father of course," said a bewildered Mrs Pearson at exactly the same time as Lady Murray said, "He is my cousin Rupert's son."

"My father was called James," objected Frances, still in a loud voice.

"Yes dear," agreed Mrs Pearson, "Henry James Metcalf. And your mother was -" For the first time she glanced across at her employer and suddenly faltered. "Wasn't she?"

"Perhaps we had better listen to her story first," suggested Lady Murray in firm tones. "The young lady was just about to tell me about herself when I asked you to come down. Tom, please bring chairs so we may all be seated."

Frances and Mrs Pearson seated themselves and Frances took up her tale again, looking from one to the other. "I was born in France, twenty four years ago of English parents. My mother's name was Amanda, Amanda Emerson I think was her maiden name and my father was James. I never knew his surname, or if I did I have forgotten it. Unfortunately mother died when I was only five years old so I do not remember very much about her. My father and I moved around a lot afterwards, and changed our names frequently so that I never knew which surname was the real one.

About six months ago, my father contracted a fatal illness, and his last instructions to me were to make my way to London and seek out Lady Julia Murray and apply to her for help. He told me to mention the name Henry Metcalf, but he was too ill to give me any further message. I came here hoping that Lady Julia would be able to provide me with an explanation, but ... here I am instead."

"It is really most unsatisfactory," Lady Murray muttered rather fretfully. She opened and shut her fan repeatedly while Frances remained silent. "If you do not know who you are, how should I?"

"Well you would if you could see her!" said Mrs Pearson, confirming what Frances had begun to suspect. Lady Murray was nearly blind.

Mrs Pearson rose to her feet and came over to Frances to give her a hug. "Welcome my dear, I did not catch your name."

"Frances, ma'am," she replied, moved by her ready affection.

"I wish I could be certain," continued Lady Murray as if Mrs Pearson had not spoken. "Do you know anything more of your parents' history? Do you have anything perhaps, belonging to them?"

"My ring. I have my father's signet ring," offered Frances, holding out her hand.

"May I?" asked Lady Murray, almost eagerly. Frances drew off the ring and put it into the outstretched hand. The old fingers moved carefully over it, "Yes. It seems like Henry's. What do you think?" she passed it to Mrs Pearson.

"I am sure it is the same one," she was more definite as she examined it closely. "The birds' wing pattern is very distinctive. How old are you again?"

"Twenty four years, ma'am."

"Well that would be about right," nodded the companion.

"What did your mother look like? Can you remember at all?" pursued Lady Murray, with some urgency.

"I was only a child," demurred Frances, "but I know she was beautiful, with long dark hair and she had grey eyes like mine. She had a lovely low singing voice too, I remember. My father missed her very much, he never remarried."

The two older ladies exchanged sudden glances, even though one could hardly see, the impulse was automatic.

"Do you know where they were married?" stepped in Mrs Pearson hastily pre-empting Lady Murray's less polite enquiry.

"Not exactly. In France I imagine, as we lived there until mother died. We were living in Nice at the time so perhaps it was there, I do not think father ever said."

"Hmph. It is not exactly straight forward, is it?" said Lady Murray quizzically, addressing the old nurse. Frances decided it was time to assert herself again.

"Let me see if I have this clear. Are you telling me that my father was your relation? Your second cousin in fact? And that his real name was Henry James Metcalf?"

"It certainly seems more than probable," agreed Lady Murray cautiously.

"But there is something else, isn't there?" probed Frances sharply, "There is some mystery or other you've not told me – and why did he live abroad under another name anyway?"

"Because of the scandal of course!" came the quick response.

"What scandal?"

"I am sorry to say that he eloped."

"Is that all? Was my mother such a mesalliance then?" exclaimed Frances in disbelief.

Provoked, Lady Murray disclosed more than she had intended. "Mesalliance? Your mother, girl, was a good cut above Henry Metcalf, let me tell you. He wasn't fit to touch the hem of her gown, and she ran away with him, deserted her friends and her family ..." the voice trailed off and she sat brooding over the past.

"How can you say that about him, your own relation?" protested Frances, hotly.

"Relation? What was that to me? Amanda was my daughter, Julia's younger sister. She was only eighteen years old."

Feeling rather dazed by these revelations, Frances murmured, "My mother was your daughter?"

Lady Murray pursed her lips and Mrs Pearson nodded. "I would say so. It appears quite clear to me that you are Henry's daughter and therefore, one supposes, Miss Amanda was your mother as they were certainly together until she died. The only time your father wrote was to inform us of that sad event. That is the problem, you see, neither of them ever told us about your birth."

Her mistress added, "There will have to be considerable investigation of course, before your claim can be accepted."

"I do not understand why you keep referring to my 'claim'," queried Frances, puzzled. "What am I supposed to be claiming?"

"Why, the money of course. If you can prove you are the oldest legitimate child of Amanda and Henry, you will be entitled to her share of the estate, about ten thousand pounds."

"Good heavens!" Ten thousand pounds! The vision of being able to meet Richard as an equal, flashed before her eyes for a second and her heart leapt. Then cold reality intruded, "I do not think I will be able to provide sufficient proof." She sighed, ten thousand pounds would have been beyond her wildest expectations.

"Why not?" queried Lady Murray sharply.

"I have no documents at all. All I have is my father's ring and that is hardly sufficient to claim a share of an estate!"

Feeling suddenly disappointed and a little depressed, Frances decided she had had enough for one day. She replaced her bonnet and took her leave.

"Thank you, my lady, for receiving me. I imagine our meeting has been as big a surprise to you as it has to me. I am sure we both have many matters to consider carefully before taking any further steps." Tucking the last strands of hair out of sight, she added, "I will bid you good day."

Both ladies were startled by her abrupt departure and Lady Murray blurted out "You are leaving then?"

"Why yes. I may call back in a couple of days if that is convenient?"

For the first time her grandmother softened towards her and became almost human, "Of course, girl. We have so much to discuss. Where are you staying? You can leave your direction with Tom if you would."

"The Regent Hotel, my lady. A message addressed to Frances White will find me."

Rather to her surprise, nobody queried this, no doubt she had given them much more significant food for thought. Tom escorted her to the door and Mrs Pearson looked as if she would have liked to have hugged her goodbye, but did not quite dare to. She contented herself with a beaming smile and Lady Murray nodded stiffly in her direction.

Her head buzzing with thoughts like a swarm of bees, Frances stepped out and into the waiting carriage. Could it all be true? Had her mother been Amanda Murray, Lady Amanda? Did she really have a grandmother, a home, a name? Smiling wryly, she decide yes to the first, she was convinced in her own mind of the truth of the relationship, but two very big question marks hung over the last two. A home? Perhaps, if Lady Murray accepted her, but a name? Well at least if it was not Metcalf it must be Murray! Little as though either of them relished the idea. Despite Mrs Pearson's intervention, Frances had known perfectly well that Lady Murray did not think her parents had been married at all!

CHAPTER 19

Meanwhile, back in Devonshire Street, Lady Anna Murray sent her footman scurrying up to the attic with orders to find and bring down all the papers left by Lady Julia. Eventually Tom descended, covered in dust and bearing two small hatboxes.

"Would these be what you were wanting, my lady?"

"Two brown hatboxes? Yes, give them to Mrs Pearson will you, Tom? You may leave us."

The old nurse was as eager as her mistress to start searching for any letter or paper which might shed some light on the circumstances surrounding Frances' birth. She blew the dust off the first box and opened it. Fearful of overlooking anything of importance, she took out each page and examined both sides before placing it on the small table beside her.

"Nothing yet, my lady, merely letters from yourself and Sir Thomas' family."

Lady Murray sat straight in her chair, her suspense betrayed only by the ceaseless opening and closing of her fan.

"There won't be anything," she declared abruptly, as Mrs Pearson came to the end of the first box. "Julia would never have kept such a matter secret from me!"

"No, my lady," responded the other woman a shade doubtfully. "Do you wish me to continue?"

"Heh? Of course continue! Can't leave the job half done!"

"No, my lady," agreed Mrs Pearson for the second time. She started on the second box. Some half hour later, she had to confess failure. "I've looked through the lot now and there's nothing here at all."

"Thought as much!" exclaimed Lady Murray with mixed satisfaction. Mrs Pearson was still unconvinced, her brow furrowed in concentration.

"Where else would she have put documents of any importance? Perhaps she considered the boxes of letters too risky, too likely to be disposed of without much attention. Did she have a safe box?" She looked up to find her employer shaking her head from side to side.

"No. All the families' important papers were lodged with Grayson's solicitors at Lincoln's Inn and they were all examined at the time of the accident."

"What happened to the rest of her things, her personal things? Are they still up in the attic?"

"I suppose they must be, I had everything packed away at the time. I have been meaning to look through it all but I have not had a spare moment."

Realising that what her ladyship really meant was that she had never been able to face that heart rending task, Mrs Pearson tactfully allowed this to pass without comment.

"I suppose you want me to sort the trunks out now? Put me to all that trouble to please that chit of a girl who is an adventuress if ever I saw one! Bold as brass, coming here like that. Nothing of her mother in her at all. She looked like Henry you say?"

"There is a very definite resemblance," stated Mrs Pearson firmly, trying to halt her employer from rushing into a position of denying Frances' claim outright. "She has his nose and his chin, and the colour of her hair is just like Henry's as a boy. I don't think there can be any doubt who her father is."

"Perhaps not," conceded Lady Murray still fighting, "but there's nothing of Amanda in her, is there?"

"Well no, not really," agreed the nurse reluctantly, "although her eyes are the same colour. There was something about her voice, I fancied it reminded me rather of someone ... not Miss Amanda exactly but ... Miss Julia! That's who! Not the accent of course, but the same low pitch, don't you think so, my lady?"

"Nonsense!" denied Lady Murray briskly, ignoring the jolt of familiarity Frances' voice had given her. "I think I've had enough excitement for the day. Perhaps we will look through those trunks another time, if the girl comes back. Now she knows she has to provide proof before she can claim the money she might give up."

"You can't deny the child her birthright just because you've taken a dislike to her," came the rather stern reply.

"No. No, if she can prove she is Amanda's child I will have to see what I can do for her. But if not, I tell you right now I will not lift a finger for Henry's bastard!" With those rather vindictive words hanging in the air, Lady Murray rose and made her way up to her chamber.

Frances returned to the Regent Hotel with her companion and was greeted by John, bursting with curiosity about her excursion to Devonshire Street.

She dismissed Madame Lebrun and then turned to her manservant with a question of her own. "How long were you with my father, John? When did you meet him?"

"In Nice it was, just after your mother died. Must be nigh on twenty years ago now. I'd got separated from the army in Spain and was working my way back to England, when your father found me, working in a livery yard, and hired me on the spot." Frances nodded, she had heard that part of the story before.

"What was he calling himself then? Can you remember?"

"James Wentworth," answered John promptly.

"Did he ever go by the name of Metcalf?"

John shook his head dubiously, "I don't remember that one. Why?"

Frances grimaced wryly, "It is just that now it appears Metcalf was his real name!" She went on to describe the rest of her afternoon, while John stared in amazement. "Her granddaughter!" he exclaimed, "Well I never!"

However, he knew as well as she did the difficulty of proving her ancestry to a solicitor.

"And even if by any remote chance, my claim could be proved, as soon as she discovers the way I have lived, Lady Murray would disown me utterly!" finished Frances, throwing up her hands. "The irony is, if I were a real adventuress which I am, this would be a perfect opportunity for me to make as much money as I could! Except of course, if I had been going about this professionally, I would have equipped myself with a better story than the one I have!"

John had been frowning in hard concentration. "I am not so sure about that, Miss Frances, after all you have told the truth so they won't be able to disprove what you have said. A simple story is the best in any case. I think you have the right of it. If they do not accept you as the legitimate heir, you will have to hold out for as big a settlement as you can, to withdraw your claim and go away."

She stared at him in dismay.

"Well what else can you do? A thousand pounds, even five hundred, would set you up nicely in France. But it may not come to that," he added bracingly. "Could we hire a solicitor of our own to make some enquiries? Find out exactly when they eloped. If your mother was a gently bred girl like that, I can't see your father travelling far without marrying her. Chances are they were married in England, before they left for France."

"Yes, I think you are right. I will consider it," she promised.

CHAPTER 20

Lord Carleton did not enjoy the next two days. He felt restless as he finalised the affairs he had set in motion and fretted over what Frances was up to in London. He still felt too uncomfortable to face Squire Herbert yet, and he actively avoided his company. Nor were things comfortable at home. Mrs Madden was very formal in her dealings with him and kept out of his way as much as possible, he was obviously still in her bad books.

His cousin Theo's return to Chatswood on his way home from York provided a welcome reprieve from the awkward atmosphere, at least until he was drawn surreptitiously aside by Mrs Madden. Theo was several years older than his cousin Richard, and the proud father of a young family. He had kept a patriarchal eye on Richard over the years and had scarcely seen anything to cause him more than a moment's anxiety and he really could not believe what Mrs Madden had told him. Richard was a grown man and he hesitated to say something to put his back up but it was too important a matter to let pass. He decided to tackle him privately after dinner.

It did not take Carleton long to realise someone, most likely Maddy, had told his cousin about Frances. Theo kept looking sideways at him and lapsing into uneasy silences, interspersed with forced conversation throughout the meal. Finally, the port was brought in and Theo said self consciously, "Got something to talk to you about, Richard."

"Yes?" queried his host invitingly.

"Not here, privately."

Carleton raised an eyebrow and said smoothly, "By all means, Theo. Let us retire to the study."

Both men seated themselves near the small fire and when Williams had carried in the decanter, Carleton dismissed him and turned to his cousin, "Problems at home, Theo?" he asked politely.

"What?" spluttered his harassed guest. "Devil take it, Richard! You know perfectly well what I need to talk to you about. What's this I hear from Maddy? I could scarce make head or tail of it!"

Carleton stared at him expressionlessly and for a moment Theo thought he wasn't going to answer him. "Maddy has been a great deal too busy!"

"'Tis only because she cares about you. Come on, Richard, don't poker up on me, what have you been up to?"

Suddenly Carleton sighed, "It sounds like a real Canterbury tale when I put it in words. I invited a recent acquaintance, a friend even, to stay with me, who was masquerading as a man but she was actually a woman, it took me some time to find that out."

Theo looked at him in total disbelief.

Carleton could not help laughing at the expression on his face. "Don't look at me like that, Theo, I am not a complete gudgeon. She managed to fool Jack Lambert and several other men of my acquaintance as well as me. She is an excellent shot with a pistol, and her sword fighting is not contemptible."

Theo realised he was gaping like a stuffed fish, "How did you meet?" he managed.

"I was being attacked by three men in the street and she saved me from losing my purse if not my life. She shot one of them in the arm." Theo did not like the admiration he heard in Richard's voice.

"You don't think it was ...?" he paused delicately.

"A scam?" answered Richard cheerfully. "No, I did wonder of course, afterwards, but I don't see how it could have been. It was only by merest chance that I was in that street at all."

"What was she doing here?" asked Theo, then suddenly flushed red, "I mean-"

"No," interrupted Richard, "it was not like that. As I said, she was here as a friend, and that is all, nothing else, Theo."

His cousin looked sceptical, "That's as maybe, Richard, but do you think anyone will believe it? Anyone else I mean?" he added hastily, seeing the frown forming on Richard's face.

"Well I don't intend to announce it to the world! In any case," he continued with studied composure, "I've offered to marry her."

Theo stared in such horror that Richard was torn between being deeply offended and going off into whoops of laughter.

"You don't need to worry, she ran away rather than take up my offer," he looked down at his waistcoat and brushed off a crumb. "More port? Or would you prefer brandy?"

Theo was speechless for a moment. It looked as if it might be worse than he had thought, Richard was obviously taken with the wench. "Eh? Oh brandy thanks."

"Will you see her again?" he ventured. "Do you know who is she?"

"I don't know," answered Carleton obscurely. "A relation of the Murrays I gather. She called herself Peter Francis when I met her." He took a sip of brandy. "I am going back to London tomorrow. Will you come with me or are you planning to stay here a few more days?"

"I will stay another day, my horses need the rest," Theo replied reluctantly, realising the subject was closed. He wondered whether he should change his plans and accompany Richard to keep an eye on him and make sure he did not do anything foolish.

Lord Carleton was up early the next morning, eager to be on his way and left immediately after he had breakfasted and made his farewells to Theo, forestalling any attempt to accompany him.

CHAPTER 21

The day after he returned to London, Carleton took a hackney to the Pelican and asked to see Peter Francis. He was still unsure exactly what he was going to say, but he was met with the news that Mr Francis had left two days ago. No, there was no forwarding address although he had mentioned visiting a cousin in Bath. Carleton guessed, correctly, that this was a red herring and left the Pelican to check if he had been seen at Manton's pistol gallery. He even managed to run into Jack Lambert at his club but a casual enquiry revealed only that Jack had not seen him since he had dropped him at the Pelican.

It was gradually dawning on him that he had no way of finding Frances if she didn't want to be found; she had no family in London and he didn't even know whether she was currently masquerading as a man or a woman. He was reluctant to involve anyone else in the search, even his man of business, but he was beginning to feel desperate. What if he never saw her again?

Lord Carleton had never thought of himself as a conceited man, but it had occurred to him, driving back to London and mulling over

what he and Theo had discussed, that perhaps he had been somewhat arrogant in presuming Frances would leap at the chance to
be his wife. When he thought back, he realised he had not actually
asked her to marry him, he had just announced his 'betrothal' to
the Squire and assumed she would agree.

He cringed inwardly as he remembered the virtuous glow he
had felt, that he was doing the honourable thing, offering to make
an honest woman of her. How patronising it must have seemed,
especially to someone as independent as Frances. If only he could
find her he would apologise and see if he could start again, court
her properly … he faltered a little at the image this conjured up, he
couldn't quite imagine Frances acting as a demure young lady. Did
she know how to dance or would she take the lead? A reluctant
smile curved his lips.

Then he wondered if she had contacted Lady Murray yet. It
seemed a distinct possibility in the light of their previous conver-
sations about her, but he could not think of an acceptable reason
for approaching Lady Murray himself to find out. He was restricted
in what enquiries he could safely make in person, without bringing
unwelcome attention on both of them. If only he had a female
relative in London that he could trust to make a call on his behalf.

Lady Murray had tried hard to put all thoughts of Frances out of
her mind but with no success. She wondered audibly if 'that girl'
would visit them again at least several times a day and eventually
Mrs Pearson took the bull by the horns and suggested they send
an invitation to her at the Regent. "Impossible!" declared Lady
Murray. "We cannot be seen to acknowledge her. At least not until
her claim is proven."

"In that case, I propose we bring Miss Julia's trunks down from the attic and start looking for any letters or papers that may be relevant. It will be a good opportunity to sort the contents out in any case," advised Mrs Pearson.

Lady Murray hemmed and hawed for another day, then conceded that perhaps it would be best to get it over with. She asked the footmen to bring a trunk down to the parlour and Mrs Pearson was soon busy unpacking clothes and sorting them into piles for sewing materials, hand-me-downs for the staff and a few costly pieces to be carefully wrapped and stored safely back in the trunk. Mrs Pearson faithfully described each article as she withdrew it and Lady Murray sat silently at first and then started to reminisce about some of the more unusual items. "I remember when Julia wore that gown to the Queen's Drawing Room, she was the most beautiful girl in the room."

"Well that's the last from that trunk," Mrs Pearson announced some time later. "No papers there. How many more trunks are there, Tom?"

"Two more, ma'am," replied the footman cautiously.

"Well, let's have them down then!" said Mrs Pearson cheerfully. She loved looking through clothes and materials. She was already planning to turn a beautiful piece of green satin into a pair of cushion covers that would match perfectly with the damask walls in the drawing room.

Tom looked hopefully at his employer, expecting a counter order, but she merely nodded and he departed for the attic with a sigh. Hopefully the next one would not be so heavy!

The second trunk proved to contain the household linen and it took scarcely any time to sort through. Most pieces were still in excellent condition and were removed to be taken upstairs by one of the maids and handed over to the housekeeper. By this time, Lady Murray was getting a little weary and told her companion to carry on without her while she went upstairs for a rest. Mrs Pearson was in full swing and merely gave a token protest, "If you are sure, my lady, I will let you know if I find anything, of course."

The third and last trunk contained coats and pantaloons that had obviously belonged to Sir Thomas. Mrs Pearson did not feel qualified to sort these and merely lifted each piece out and shook it to determine that nothing had been hidden between the folds. Eventually this task was completed and the articles of clothing returned to the trunk.

She turned to the footman despondently, "Was that it then, Tom? Are you sure?" She had been so certain she had been going to find some papers or even a letter from Amanda hidden away.

"There is nothing else ma'am," he assured her. "Well, apart from a few pieces of furniture of course."

"Furniture? What kind of furniture?"

"Just a desk ma'am, and a little dressing table-like thing," he answered doubtfully. "Perhaps you would like to come up and have a look for yourself?"

Mrs Pearson nodded then sighed as she got to her feet. "Perhaps later, Tom. I am feeling a little tired myself. Please ask Annie to come in and I'll tell her where all these things need to go. The trunks can go back in the attic now, thank you."

The parlour was soon restored to its normal state and Mrs Pearson went upstairs herself for a brief rest before dinner. The furniture would still be there tomorrow.

Frances meanwhile was oblivious of the concern she was caus-
ing in other quarters. She had taken John's advice, and hired a
solicitor to investigate the time and place of her parents' marriage,
twenty five years ago. While she was waiting for the results,
she took the opportunity to refurbish her female wardrobe and
to purchase such things as face powder, a new wig and other
accessories. Her hair was starting to lengthen, as she had not cut
it for several weeks, but it would be some time before it was at an
acceptably feminine length. She started to venture forth on small
outings to the park and the circulating library but was careful to
act as decorously as possible in case Lady Murray was having her
watched.

For a while she had debated whether or not to start calling
herself Frances Metcalf, but in the end decided against it. She did
not want to antagonise Lady Murray further at this stage, although
if she could not find any proof to support her claim she might have
to change her strategy.

Unfortunately her quiet period of reflection also allowed her
plenty of time to think about Lord Carleton. She missed him and
wondered what he was doing and whether he thought of her at all.
More than once she was tempted to dress as Peter again and seek
him out but she knew this would be fatal to her plans. She made
a bargain with herself that she would not try and see him again
until she was accepted by Lady Murray, she was not sure what she
would do if the plan failed. Did she love him enough, or too much,
to become his mistress? Providing he still wanted her of course.

CHAPTER 22

Mrs Pearson dressed in her oldest clothes to brave the attic, she suspected, rightly as it turned out, that it had not been dusted in some time. Tom accompanied her and showed her which few pieces of furniture stored there had belonged to Lady Julia. There was a beautiful, polished writing table with patterns of mother of pearl inlaid on the drawers, a delicate white painted dressing table with gilt trim and, under a dust cloth, was a chaise longue made of rosewood with cream satin cushions.

"If there are any papers here they will be in the desk or the dressing table," mused Mrs Pearson, opening the two larger drawers in the dressing table as she spoke. They were empty however, the brushes and cosmetics obviously removed before the piece was brought to Lady Murray's house. The small drawers mounted on each side of the dressing table were also empty.

She turned to the writing desk and found that several of the drawers were locked. This looked promising and she hunted eagerly until she found the small key. Triumphantly she drew forth the small bundle of letters tied with pink ribbon, only to find after a brief glance that they were love letters from Sir Thomas. Hastily she returned them, a slight blush on her cheeks, who would have thought Sir Thomas was so romantic?

Eventually she found a small puzzle box at the back of one of the drawers. How did it open? She tried pushing several sections of wood without success and put it aside to take down to Lady Anna. There were no other papers in the desk. She picked up the puzzle box and made her way carefully down stairs, followed by Tom, thankful that he hadn't been asked to carry down any of the furniture.

Her employer was seated in the morning salon, waiting for her return. "Well?"

"Lady Anna? Do you remember how to open the puzzle box? I found it in Lady Julia's writing desk and I think it is the same one she had as a child." Mrs Pearson put it carefully into Lady Anna's outstretched hands.

"Let me see," she murmured, her fingers sliding over the wood. It was shaped like a small row of books in a bookshelf. "I think I have it." The bottom shelf slid to the left, allowing the books, which were in one piece to rotate clockwise, in turn exposing a small keyhole. "Do we have the key?" she asked.

"I do not think so," answered Mrs Pearson regretfully. "It certainly was not in the desk. What shall we do?"

"Tom? Do you think you can open it with a knife?" asked Lady Murray.

"I can try, my lady," said Tom doubtfully. "I'll be back in a minute." He returned shortly carrying a small kitchen knife, "Will you hand it to me, my lady?" He fiddled with the point of the blade for a few minutes, "I think I'll have to break the lock, my lady."

She nodded and in a few seconds the box was open. Tom gave it to Mrs Pearson and she carefully withdrew the tightly folded papers from inside. "It looks like two letters, Lady Anna. Shall I read them?" With her employer directly in front of her she felt obliged to ask permission, even as her fingers were already unfolding the thin paper.

"Go ahead."

Mrs Pearson gave a gasp as her eyes flew ahead to the signature at the bottom. "It is from Miss Amanda, my lady!"

Lady Murray pursed her lips tightly, "You may leave us Tom." She would have given anything to have been able to dismiss her companion as well and read the letters alone but she needed her eyes. Although she could distinguish between light and dark, she certainly could not see enough to read.

"My dearest Julia,

I hope this finds you well. My beautiful baby has arrived safely. She takes after Henry, she has his hair but my eyes. We have christened her Frances Julia Metcalf, although we are not using that name here in France of course! My health is not yet what it should be, but the doctor says I should regain my strength if I do not do too much. Easy for him to say! I have written to Mother but I do not know if she will even open my letter, you know how bitterly we parted and she has not forgiven me. I hope the birth of her granddaughter may change her heart. My dearest sister I miss you so much and although I am homesick for England, my baby gives me great joy. Henry sends his warmest regards,

Your loving sister Amanda"

Mrs Pearson stopped reading to wipe a tear from her eye and looked at Lady Murray's closed face.

'We must keep this to ourselves for a while," she ordered. "I need to consider what this means."

"But surely," faltered Mrs Pearson, "It means you have a grand-daughter ... doesn't it?"

"It would certainly appear so, but whether she is legitimate or not is still uncertain. What is in the other letter?" she asked.

Her companion looked down as she unfolded the second sheet of paper.

"My dear Julia

I write this to you at the request of our beloved Amanda. I have sad news. Her health has not improved as we had hoped and the doctor says she has not long now. She sends you her love and hopes for a happy and fulfilling life for you. We received your letter at Christmas and it was the source of much pleasure to her. We have not heard a word from your mother. Amanda tells me she has forgiven her but I cannot – however I will say no more. I hope one day we will be able to return to England and you will be able to meet your niece who is growing more beautiful and more delightful every day. I hope this finds you in good health,

Your loving brother and sister,

Henry and Amanda"

Tears were running down Mrs Pearson's cheeks as she finished, and it took a while for Lady Murray's next words to penetrate.

"Burn it!"

"Pardon me?" Surely she had misheard.

"You heard me, throw it on the fire!" Lady Murray made as if to snatch the paper from the old nurse's hands. Not really aware of why she did it, Mrs Pearson tucked the letter quickly into her reticule, then she leant forward and audibly stoked up the fire. "There, it is done," she lied.

Hastily she checked that she had the other letter safe. Yes, there it was. She tucked that inside her reticule as well. "I think I will go upstairs and have a rest, my lady. Shall I call Annie to you?"

"Yes, thank you, Maria. Remember what I said, not a word to anyone yet," Lady Murray emphasised.

"Of course not, my lady."

For the first time, Mrs Pearson wondered if Lady Murray had in fact received the letters sent by her daughter but had chosen to ignore them. She knew she was high in the instep but to put respectability and propriety before family was something Mrs Pearson could not understand.

Meanwhile Lady Murray was weighing her options. She decided it was time to call in her solicitor, he had as vested an interest as she did in making sure Frances was not accepted as a legitimate heir and paid out her ten thousand pounds. She summoned Hanson, her butler, to send a message to Mr Pilkington asking him to call at his earliest convenience. There was no legal proof of anything so far, she would simply stand firm and deny the relationship, but it would be better if Mrs Pearson was not involved in this, she was too sentimental. Would it be possible to see that she was sent on a short holiday?

Mrs Madden did not know what to do. She was sincerely shocked and distressed by the goings on of the last week at Chatswood. She had known there was something shady about Francis from the beginning, at first she thought he was there merely to hang on Richard's coattails but then she grew increasingly uncomfortable at the insidious way he was worming his way into Richard's confidence.

When she overheard the squire's exclamation in the study she had been absolutely horrified to learn that Frances was a woman. How dared Richard bring his light o' love to his home, to parade around in breeches in front of everyone? She was obviously completely shameless. She must have bewitched him, Lord Carleton had always behaved with dignity and propriety until now but he was clearly infatuated with the strumpet. What could she do to save him from himself?

She attempted to approach Theo with her concerns but he refused to discuss Richard with her, "Leave it be, Maddy. Richard is a grown man, he'll not appreciate you meddling in his affairs."

But if she didn't, who else would? That was when the name of Lady Anna Murray popped into her head. Frances was apparently some sort of relation, if Lady Murray, a high stickler by all accounts, knew about her behaviour she would be certain to take drastic measures to control her. Mrs Madden vacillated for a while but finally decided it was her duty to protect Richard. She went upstairs to her room and sat down at her little writing desk.

"My dear Lady Murray,

I am writing to you to tell you about the wanton behaviour of the person who goes by the name of Frances. I understand she is a connection of yours. She dresses in male attire and recently spent a week at the house of Lord Richard Carleton, as his close companion! I do not need to tell you the scandal this would cause if it became known. I hope you can do something about this,

Yours sincerely,

A friend"

Before she could reconsider, she folded the paper, addressed and sealed it, and put it in her reticule to post when she was next in Guildford. A couple of days later she posted the letter feeling virtuous, she had done all she could, now it was out of her hands. Richard would never have to know.

CHAPTER 23

Unaware of the schemes being hatched against her, Frances continued to live quietly at the Regent while she waited for a report from her solicitor and his enquiry agent. She went for brisk walks in the park accompanied by long suffering Madame Lebrun and also paid several visits to the British Museum. They both enjoyed occasional browses through Grafton House, picking up bargains.

John had disappeared on his own business as she did not require his services while she was staying at the hotel. In fact, John had gone to visit the area in Kent where Amanda Murray had grown up and eloped with Henry Metcalf. He thought he might have some luck talking to the older inhabitants of Sevenoaks village, and at least, attempt to determine the route they would have likely taken to the coast. He was fairly certain they would have departed England at Dover, but his own theory was that Henry would have married her as soon as possible after leaving Sevenoaks.

He visited both inns and the local shops, seeking older folk prepared to have a chat and reminisce about the past. He stated openly that he had been in service with Mr Henry, when he found that the villagers still had a soft spot for him. He also spoke briefly to the rector but was not surprised to get a cool reception from him as he was beholden to Lady Murray for his livelihood. The word soon spread that Mr Henry's man was seeking information about him and he found himself approached by several persons eager to find out what Mr Henry had been up to since he went to France.

They were dismayed, but not surprised to learn that he had died abroad but absolutely flabbergasted to hear that he had a daughter even now in England. It became apparent that although Lady Murray was respected, she was not particularly liked by the local villagers, and few thought it odd that she had never mentioned having a granddaughter.

John stayed a couple of nights at the most comfortable inn, waiting for the news of his search to spread and hoping for a visit from someone who could help him. He was sitting over a tankard of ale the evening of the third day when an elderly man with a wizened face like a walnut came and sat next to him. "You were with Mr Henry?"

John nodded. "Nigh on twenty years."

"Longish time that."

"Ale?" at the answering nod, John gestured to the serving maid.

"Now I'm in service to Miss Frances, his daughter," John continued after they were both served another foaming tankard. "To be honest, there's some question as to whether her parents were wed and I'm here to try and find out. From what I knew of Mr Henry, it doesn't seem likely that he would've just run off with a young lady like that."

The other man was nodding, "I reckon you're right there, he liked kicking up a lark but there weren't no harm in him. You might do worse than to try the rector over at St Martin's, in Brasted."

"Brasted? That's to the west isn't it? Further away from the coast?"

"Aye 'tis that, but seems he and Mr Henry were at Oxford together." He gave John a steady look as he spoke.

"Ah." John nodded. "Another?"

They moved on to talk about some of Henry's adventures abroad, John gradually gathering a small but interested crowd around him.

The next morning, John rode off to Brasted, his head slightly the worse for wear. He soon spotted the square tower of St Martin's above the rest of the village and made his way there. The church was unlocked and he entered cautiously. A middle aged woman who was sweeping the floor, directed him to the rectory, "Rector's name is Mr Thomas, sir," she added. "He should be there at this time of day."

John walked over to the rectory, a low red brick building with a tiled roof and a neat garden out the front. He knocked at the door and was answered by the rector himself. "Yes? What can I do for you?" Mr Thomas had a pleasant open face and was clad in a black coat which gaped slightly over a comfortable stomach.

"Good morning, sir, I was wondering if I might talk to you about my late master, Mr Henry Metcalf."

"Good heavens!" Mr Thomas exclaimed, "I haven't heard that name in years! Do come in, my good fellow, and tell me what happened to him."

John entered the vicarage and was led into the parlour and asked to take a seat. He gave Mr Thomas a brief summary of the last twenty years and then led into the reason for his visit.

"You see, sir, I am the only person Miss Frances has to look out for her interests since her father passed away. She has been to visit Lady Murray who told her that if she can prove she is their legitimate daughter she stands to inherit ten thousand pounds. However Lady Murray is not convinced Lady Amanda and Mr Henry ever married, so I thought I would come here and do some investigating of my own. A chap I met in the village at Sevenoaks directed me to you. So here I am. Can you help me?"

"How extraordinary! Of course they were married. Henry had a special licence and I married them myself. I find it hard to believe Lady Murray did not know that." Mr Thomas was dumbfounded.

John looked at him in disbelief, how could it have been that easy? Brasted was only five miles from Sevenoaks, Lady Murray had certainly not looked very far to find out if her daughter had been married or not! Together, they went across to the church and the rector got out the parish registry and showed John the entry. "Here it is, you can see for yourself."

"Amanda Louise Emerson Murray (spinster) and Henry James Metcalf (bachelor)," John read aloud.

"Here," offered the rector, "If you can wait a moment I shall write a letter confirming this for you to take to Miss Frances."

John thanked him profusely. It all seemed too easy. He was never quite sure what made him cautious, but he asked politely, "Would you mind very much sir, writing me two letters? Then Miss Frances can give one to Lady Murray," and still have her own copy, he thought, just in case anything happens to the first one.

This was no trouble and soon John was on his way back to Sevenoaks after making a modest contribution to the church roof fund, the two letters tucked safely inside his jacket. He debated with himself whether to keep the news secret or not but in the end decided that the more who knew the better.

"Yes, they were married in Brasted by special licence," he announced to the landlord on his return. "I shall be on my way back to London now to give Miss Frances the news. I have a letter from the rector and all to prove it." He was certain the report would spread like wildfire. Now let Lady Murray deny Miss Frances was her granddaughter!

CHAPTER 24

It was fourteen days since he had seen Frances, Lord Carleton had counted every one of them. His feelings for her were growing stronger rather than fading away with the passing of time, the young girls on display in the Marriage Mart seemed pale and uninteresting compared to Frances. He realised reluctantly that she was not going to contact him and he was not going to find her by himself, so he at last approached his man of business for help.

He concluded that she was currently presenting herself as a woman because he had not seen or heard of Peter Francis in any of his usual haunts since his return to London, and he asked Mr Adams to send one of his clerks to each respectable hotel with a delivery of artificial flowers, to enquire if they had anyone with the name of "Frances" staying with them. At least the name was sufficiently unusual that there were not likely to be many.

John felt a mixture of excitement and rather undefined anxiety as he rode back to London. He should be feeling pure happiness that Frances would be able to come into her inheritance and take her rightful place in society, but perhaps years of working with a gamester who knew that when things seemed too good to be true there was usually a reason, had instilled wariness in him.

Frances was overjoyed when he gave her the letter and told her about his meeting with the rector at St Martin's. Now I can contact Richard, was her immediate unspoken response but she said. "This is wonderful, John! I must visit Lady Murray as soon as possible to give her this."

"Hold yer horses," cautioned her retainer. "Perhaps you should call on that solicitor of yours first, let him make the arrangements. Lady Murray might not be so happy as you think with this turn of events."

"I am sure you are wrong, John. She might be a trifle crusty, but she is family after all." Frances was too happy to listen to sober counsel and asked John to arrange for a hackney to take her to Devonshire Street. She changed into her best morning dress and whisked Madame Lebrun off with her to visit her newly acquired grandmother. John made sure he had the second copy of the rector's letter tucked safely inside his jerkin. He had a bad feeling about this.

It appeared that his fears were groundless. Frances was admitted to the morning salon where Mrs Pearson had been reading to Lady Murray. They looked up as she entered, Mrs Pearson smiling tentatively and Lady Murray schooling her face with a polite expression of enquiry.

"Good morning, my lady, Mrs Pearson. I am sorry to burst in on you like this but I have some great news!" enthused Frances. "It will be a relief I think, for you to know that your daughter, my mother, was properly wed to my father. My servant found the record in the parish register at Brasted. Here, I have a letter for you from the rector," she placed it into Mrs Pearson's trembling hand.

"My goodness!" she exclaimed, "That is wonderful isn't it?" She turned to her employer, who just had time to paste a pleased expression on her face, before answering graciously, "Yes indeed."

"Just think! Brasted!" Mrs Pearson continued to wonder and exclaim, innocently covering the fact that Lady Murray sat in silence as her brain rushed to consider how best to deal with the situation.

"You must come and stay with us, my dear," she announced suddenly, it would be best to have the girl under her charge while she decided what to do.

"Yes," agreed Mrs Pearson enthusiastically, "I will have a room prepared immediately. You must make your home with us now, Frances."

"Well I will certainly come for a visit," Frances answered, feeling a little startled by the offer. Her more cautious self was suddenly waking up, did she really want to live with Lady Murray and be subject to her notions of what was suitable for her? If she moved into Devonshire Street she would be forsaking most of her independence. There would be no more dressing in male attire, no more shooting or fencing, she would not even be able to leave the house without a companion.

They talked for a little longer then Frances took her leave to return to the hotel and make arrangements. "Surely I can send a servant to do that for you?" suggested Lady Murray.

"Thank you, my lady, but there are some matters I must attend to personally," replied Frances, her heart sinking as she realised the restrictions she would now be faced with on a daily basis.

She returned to the Regent Hotel, impatient to tell John what had occurred. He agreed reluctantly that she needed to at least visit with Lady Murray, but encouraged her to continue renting the rooms at the Regent for another week or two so that she would have somewhere to go if affairs did not go smoothly. Frances felt obliged to fulfil her bargain with Madame Lebrun. She dismissed her with an extra week's wages and gave her the money for her fare to Paris as previously agreed. Madame was effusive in her thanks, but ventured to ask if she was sure she would be able to manage without her.

They decided that John would continue to stay at the Regent until she made more permanent plans, he would hardly fit in at Devonshire Street. Before she packed a bag, containing only her female clothes and accessories, Frances sat down to write a letter to Lord Carleton. John would deliver it to him after he had dropped her at Devonshire Street.

"My dear Carleton,

I have been waiting until I sorted out my affairs before con-tacting you again. I have a name now, Frances Metcalf. I am the daughter of Lady Amanda Murray and Henry Metcalf and they were married at Brasted in Kent, twenty five years ago. I have approached my grandmother Lady Murray and she has invited me to stay with her until my inheritance is arranged, I have been told I am to inherit ten thousand pounds! It all seems like a fairy tale and best of all it is true and not a scam!

I must tell you why I left Chatswood as I did, though perhaps you have guessed the reason yourself by now! I did not want to trap you into offering for an adventuress, your unfailing kindness to me did not deserve to be repaid in that manner. I hope in time you will find yourself able to forgive me,

Yours sincerely

Frances Metcalf"

It was not exactly what she wanted to write, but she did not want to appear too forward; after all, Carleton may have felt glad to be rid of her. She felt she had owed him an explanation, even at the risk of placing her future in his hands if he wanted to destroy her. He was the only person in London, apart from John, who knew her whole story. She was already inventing a heavily edited version to tell Lady Murray and Mrs Pearson, without actually gammoning them too much.

Eventually she was packed, made her farewells to Madame Lebrun, who would leave in the morning to take the stage to Dover, and left sufficient funds with John to allow him to stay at the Regent for some weeks. She also left her male attire, including her pistol, securely locked in a bag in her room. Then she was off to Devonshire Street and a new chapter in her life.

CHAPTER 25

F rances followed Mrs Pearson upstairs to a delightful room, furnished in pale blue. A young girl followed them silently. "This is Annie, she will be your maid until you find someone yourself," advised the older woman. "I will leave you to get settled; then, when you are ready, Annie will bring you down to the parlour for tea. Oh I am so glad to see you here, I was your mother's nurse you know."

"You must tell me all about her," responded Frances, "I would love to hear your stories, in fact I know very little about this side of my family at all."

"I am sure the two of us will have lots of opportunities for a comfortable cose. Lady Murray does not like to remember the past," she explained carefully.

Annie was young, with light brown hair tucked under a cap, and slightly blotchy skin. Deftly she unpacked Frances' bags and put things away, without saying a word. "Thank you, Annie," said Frances, and she dipped her head and smiled shyly.

"Can you show me the parlour, please?" The maid led her down-stairs to a small room decorated with white and gold panelling and delicately carved chairs. Lady Murray was already seated and called for the tea tray when Frances arrived. Expecting to give an account of how she had spent her life, Frances was taken aback when Lady Murray's first question was, "What accomplishments do you have girl? Maria, Mrs Pearson that is, says you have the look of a lady, and your voice is acceptable, but what are your accomplishments?"

"I am afraid I do not have many, your ladyship. I sew a little of course but I do not play an instrument, or sketch. However, I speak French and Italian fluently, and German, a little." Frances answered honestly. She resisted the temptation to add that she could also fence a little and out shoot most men, though it would almost have been worth it to wipe the condescending smile off Lady Murray's face.

"I feared as much. What about dancing?"

"I am familiar with some country dances, but a few lessons to teach me the current steps would be helpful." She replied, trying hard not to let her offense show.

Lady Murray smiled suddenly, "You will forgive me if I do not introduce you to society just yet. You will need proper clothes and dancing lessons at least before we present you. I am sure you will feel more comfortable with that, rather than to be thrust into a round of activities too soon."

Frances had rather been looking forward to engaging in a round of social activities, but she could hardly gainsay her grandmother, and murmured a polite "Thank you, my lady." A small spark of rebellion prompted her to add innocently, "Should I call you Grandmere, or Grandmama, my lady?"

Lady Murray suppressed a wince. "You may call me Grandmother," she conceded reluctantly, she could hardly insist the girl keep calling her Lady Murray! "Maria has a good eye for fashion, she can take you to my dressmaker tomorrow. I will ask her to look through your wardrobe and see if anything you have is suitable for your new station."

Frances bit her lip, there was no point in taking umbrage. She would just have to pretend she was undertaking a new masquerade for the period of her visit, that of demure young lady. She wondered how soon she could lay hands on her ten thousand pounds and set up her own establishment. Fortunately Lady Murray retired to her room shortly afterwards for a rest, and Frances went upstairs with Mrs Pearson to look through her wardrobe and discuss what new clothes she would need to purchase tomorrow.

Lord Carleton was beginning to think he was the victim of a malicious fate. No sooner had his plan succeeded, and Frances been located by his agent's clerk at the Regent Hotel, than she disappeared again before he could talk to her. He arrived home feeling discouraged, to find a letter had been left for him in his absence. He unfolded it half heartedly, then drew in his breath as he recognised who it was from. Eagerly he scanned the short missive.

"My dear Carleton,

I have been waiting until I sorted out my affairs before contacting you again. I have a name now, Frances Metcalf. I am the daughter of Lady Amanda Murray and Henry Metcalf and they were married at Brasted in Kent, twenty five years ago. I have approached my grandmother Lady Murray and she has invited me to stay with her until my inheritance is arranged, I have been told I am to inherit ten thousand pounds! It all seems like a fairy tale and best of all it is true and not a scam!

I must tell you why I left Chatswood as I did, though perhaps you have guessed the reason yourself by now! I did not want to trap you into offering for an adventuress, your unfailing kindness to me did not deserve to be repaid in that manner. I hope in time you will find yourself able to forgive me,

Yours sincerely

Frances Metcalf"

He read it a second time. Did she want him to seek her out or not? It certainly sounded as if she cared for him but whether it was as a friend or something warmer he could not tell. He needed a private conversation with her, but how could he approach her at Lady Murray's residence without admitting a prior acquaintance? As far as he was aware, no-one outside Lady Murray's immediate household even knew of her existence yet.

He would have to wait until she was introduced socially to the ton and then seek an introduction, he must curb his impatience. For the first time, he wished she was still masquerading as Peter Francis, it would certainly have been a lot easier to arrange a meeting.

Frances and Mrs Pearson greatly enjoyed their expedition to Lady Murray's dressmaker the following day. They ordered two evening gowns, a muslin dress gathered high above the waist to wear in the day time, a pelisse with velvet trim and a blue bonnet to match and felt very extravagant.

While they were out, a letter was delivered to Lady Murray and she asked Hanson to read it to her. She was exceedingly glad she had not waited for Mrs Pearson to return when he opened the letter, and after glancing at it, suggested in a wooden voice that they move to the privacy of the parlour.

"My dear Lady Murray,

I am writing to you tell you about the wanton behaviour of the person who goes by the name of Frances. I understand she is a connection of yours. She dresses in male attire and recently spent a week at the house of Lord Richard Carleton, as his close companion! I do not need to tell you the scandal this would cause if it became known. I hope you can do something about this,

Yours sincerely,

A friend"

Lady Murray felt a curious mixture of horror and vindication, "I knew something like this would happen!" she said harshly. "There was bad blood in Henry and it has come out in the daughter. She must be mad!" she concluded with certainty. "The girl obviously needs to be looked after, she is not capable of keeping herself decent."

She thought for a moment, "Send for Mr Pilkington immediately, Hanson, I will get him to investigate this. Also, I think we should ask Dr Russell to call tomorrow. I fancy his services will be required to keep her under control. Arrange it will you? Mind, not a word to anyone else, especially Mrs Pearson - I will break the sad news to her myself, she will be very distressed."

"Yes, my lady. What shall I do with the letter?"

"Give it to me. I will need to show Mr Pilkington." Lady Murray took the letter and held it carefully, it was the most valuable thing she had received for ages. She waited impatiently for Mr Pilkington who, fortunately for both of them, was not busy when Hanson called and was able to return with him in the hackney.

"I have received some interesting news about my granddaughter," she told him calmly, passing him the letter. "You may find this will be of assistance to us."

Her solicitor took the letter gingerly and quickly skimmed it. "Yes indeed, my lady, very interesting, if true," he added suavely.

"That's what I want you to investigate for me, privately of course. I do not want this to be known outside these four walls, at least not yet!"

He nodded and bowed himself out of the room, "At once, my lady."

She went slowly upstairs to her room, plans forming in her head only to be discarded as she realised their weaknesses; her scheme needed to be foolproof. Surely she had some laudanum handy? She would make sure Hanson arranged for some to be put in Frances' morning cup of hot chocolate, that would keep her docile until Dr Russell arrived and she could put the rest of her scheme into place.

The two shoppers returned to the house, unaware of the disaster looming over their heads. Lady Murray remained in her room, she did not think she could manage to treat Frances with civility and pleaded a headache when Mrs Pearson went up to enquire. "I shall just rest here quietly, Maria, but please come up and see me before you retire for the night," she requested in a faint voice.

Mrs Pearson knocked lightly on her door later that night after Frances had retired, and was bid to enter. Lady Murray was propped up in her bed and turned a tragic face towards her old companion. "Maria, you must prepare yourself for terrible news," she turned a searching gaze upon her and patted the side of the bed. "Be seated, I have had a great shock. Our Frances is not ... not well" her voice faltered convincingly.

"My lady, what on earth has happened?" cried Mrs Pearson anxiously.

"While you were out this afternoon, I had a visit from Mr Pilkington." Lady Murray thought correctly that this would carry more weight than an anonymous letter. "He has been looking into the girl's history for me, to see if we could verify her claim and unfortunately he made a terrible discovery. Before she came to us she was living with a man!"

She continued, over Mrs Pearson's gasp of horror. "Not only has she lost her virtue but I fear she has been seen wearing men's clothes in public. I can only conclude that she is suffering from an inflammation of the brain, so I have asked if Dr Russell might call as a matter of urgency tomorrow. We will see what can be done, perhaps a quiet life in the country ..."

"Good heavens! What are we to do? I cannot believe it, is Mr Pilkington certain of his facts?" Mrs Pearson was devastated.

"Unfortunately it is all too true," Lady Murray sighed. "We will see what can be done tomorrow, after I have seen Dr Russell. I know I shall not sleep a wink tonight but we must get what rest we can. Good night, Maria, I am sure I do not need to tell you, but not a word to the girl until Dr Russell has been, I will talk to her myself after I have decided what to do."

"Of course, my lady, oh I cannot believe it!" she exclaimed again. Not only had Mrs Pearson become fond of Frances but she had been eagerly looking forward to presenting her to their friends and the round of social activities this would entail. Grateful as she was to Lady Murray for providing her with a home and a comfortable life, sometimes it did all seem rather quiet, not to say dull. A lively young person was just what they needed, she had thought.

Sadly she went to her room, only to lie on her bed, tossing and turning, unable to sleep. After a while her natural optimism began to reassert itself. Perhaps it was not quite as bad as Lady Murray feared, she was always one to see the worst side of things. Who was the man involved? Perhaps if he were not totally unacceptable he could marry Frances and make her, if not respectable, at least less scandalous.

CHAPTER 26

Unsuspecting, Frances woke early as usual the next morning and drank her cup of hot chocolate, grimacing a little at the taste, perhaps the milk was not quite fresh today. She had almost finished dressing before the effects of the laudanum began to overtake her and she felt sleepy and a bit dizzy.

"I think I must have caught a chill or something yesterday, Annie, I really don't feel at all well. Perhaps I had better go back to bed for a while, could you please apologise to Lady Murray for me?" Annie helped take off her dress and she lay back down on the bed, then fell into an uneasy dose.

When she awoke some hours later she could not think where she was. She was certainly not in her blue bedroom. She looked around groggily, what the deuce? There was a doll in a crib by the window and a miniature set of chairs in front of the fireplace, it looked as if she was in the nursery. She was lying tucked up in a narrow bed with a white cotton cover, but apart from the children's playthings there was nothing else in the room.

Shakily she got out of bed and went to the door. She looked down disbelievingly, it was locked. "Hello?" she called uncertainly, was she dreaming? There was no sound from the other side of the door and she went to the window and looked out through the bars. Bars? Of course there were bars, she realised, it was a nursery.

Frances was starting to get alarmed and a little angry. Who on earth was playing this trick on her? She knocked loudly on the door, "Hullo? Is anyone there?" she called again.

She continued knocking and shouting for five minutes but there was no response. Eventually she gave up for the moment and looked around the room more thoroughly. It did not take long, there was no furniture other than the bed. Gradually she became aware that she was wearing her camisole and drawers but there were no other clothes in the room. There was however a chamber pot under the bed. She was still feeling rather queasy, so she decided the most sensible thing to do was to lie back down on the bed and wait for whoever it was to come back and tell her what was happening.

Frances had fallen back into a light doze when the door opened and Lady Murray came in accompanied by Tom who was looking both fearful and embarrassed.

"What is the meaning of this?" she demanded, instantly awake.

"You are being confined, for your own safety," replied Lady Murray bluntly. "Your behaviour has been such that I can no longer allow you to leave the house. Dr Russell advised that it would be best if you were removed to a quiet place in the country but until we can arrange that you will remain in this room."

"What in heavens' name are you talking about? What behaviour?" Frances was flabbergasted.

"Your wantoness, your complete lack of modesty and virtue! I have received a letter from Chatswood – ah I see you know what that means! You have been exposed as nothing but a strumpet!" Lady Murray struggled to control herself. "I am certain you must be suffering from a brain fever. Dr Russell has seen you and he agrees with me, however, no relation of mine shall be placed in Bedlam, not even you. A quiet life in the country is the best you can hope for. If you are wise, you will agree with me on this, it will make things so much more pleasant for you."

She smiled grimly. "Dr Russell has left me some medicine for you in case you should become violent, I hope I will not have to use it. I will leave you now. If you are quiet and obedient, Tom will bring you something to eat and drink in a little while, and possibly a book to read."

Frances was too shocked to react when Lady Murray whisked out of the room with Tom behind her and locked the door again. She felt like banging on the door and screaming her head off but she sat down bemusedly on the bed. Think, I must think, not react hysterically, which is what they are expecting I am sure. Perhaps I will play their game for awhile, pretend to capitulate, and wait for an opportunity to escape.

Mrs Pearson was dithering. When she had asked Lady Murray if she could pop up and see Frances she had been told that at the moment it would be too unsettling for her to have visitors, perhaps in a day or two it might be possible.

Although Lady Murray had spoken as if she were distressed when she talked about Frances, her companion was no longer certain that was the truth. She noticed she had stopped using her name. Instead she called her 'that girl' and more than once she had caught a look of triumph on her face which she had been unable to understand. She remembered how bitter had been the breach between Lady Amanda and her mother, how long Lady Murray had held the grudge, was she perhaps now extending it to Frances? Mrs Pearson was certain Amanda would have wanted her to help her daughter if she could. She did not like to disobey her employer but she felt she must see Frances for herself and talk to her.

Waiting until Lady Murray had retired for the night and the house was quiet, Mrs Pearson crept upstairs to the nursery. There was a light in the passage! She stopped at the corner and peered around. She could not believe her eyes, Tom was sitting slumped in a chair in front of the door, giving the strong and unpleasant suggestion of a jailer. Quickly she tiptoed back to her room, something havey-cavey was definitely going on!

John Hopgood was also feeling uneasy about the situation, Frances had not been in touch for several days and this was unlike her. He hunted around for a reason to call on her and discovered a single glove lying forgotten under her bed. He took this, dressed himself in a clean jacket and went around to the servants' entrance of the house on Devonshire Street.

"Please be so good as to tell Miss Frances I am here, I'm Hopgood," he told the young maid who opened the door to him. The girl gave him an odd look and said, "I'll just get Mr Hanson." She returned in a moment with a superior looking man in a frock coat, "And you are?" he asked coldly.

"Miss Frances' manservant," replied John, not liking the look of things at all. He held up the glove.

"You may leave it with me," said the butler. "You may go. The lady in question no longer needs your services, my good man."

"But I must see her!" demanded John. "What about my wages? She still owes me two weeks wages."

The butler frowned at him, "Wait here." He disappeared into the house and returned with ten shillings. "Take this and go, or I will call the constable," he ordered.

"There's no need for that, me fine fellow," said John, taking the money. "I just want what's owing to me." He sauntered off without a backward glance.

There was something very wrong here, he had told Frances it was all too good to be true, but she hadn't listened, and now she was in a right scrape. He needed help, a fancy house like that, there was no way he could get inside. For a moment he imagined what would happen if he went to the Runners and told them a young woman was being held there against her will. They would think he was telling them a Canterbury Tale, either that, or he was in his cups. No-one would believe him.

CHAPTER 27

Lord Carleton was the third person to have his peace cut up that evening, worrying about Frances. He had heard absolutely nothing since he received her letter. The news of a lost heiress returned to the fold should have flown around London's drawing rooms before the gossips could have drawn a second breath. The silence was deafening, and more than a little disquieting. He would have to take the bull by the horns and call on Lady Murray tomorrow. Perhaps he could say he had known Frances' father and wished to pay his respects to his daughter?

He was just about to set out for his club for a late supper, when his butler drew himself to his attention by appearing at his elbow and clearing his throat.

"Excuse me, my lord, but there is a person here to see you," he said cautiously. "I explained that you were about to go out and suggested he call back tomorrow but he was very insistent. He said you would think it important. His name is Hopgood but he said that would not likely mean anything to you, so he asked me to give you this letter."

Carleton had been looking at him with raised eyebrows but took the folded piece of paper held out to him. It was from the rector of Brasted announcing the fact that he had married Lady Amanda Murray to Mr Henry Metcalf twenty five years ago. Frances! Carleton seized the butler's arm. "Quickly, man, where is he?"

"In the hall, my lord," stuttered Rawlings in alarm. Carleton released him and strode down to the hall where a middle aged stranger was standing, twisting his cap between his hands. The disappointment was like a blow.

"Yes?" he asked, unaware of how intimidating he looked in his evening wear, his cloak already around his shoulders.

The older man gazed hesitantly up at him, was this tall, elegant Corinthian really a friend of Frances? Well he had come this far, he wasn't going to give up without a struggle.

He stated in a firm voice, "I've come about Miss Frances, milord," then stopped as Carleton held up his hand and shook his head slightly. The change in Carleton's face was remarkable, it was as if someone had turned on a light. "Let us go into the study, Hopgood, is it?"

"Yes, my lord," he answered bemusedly as he was ushered into a cosy study and seated in a leather chair before he could blink.

"That will be all, Rawlings, thank you." Carleton dismissed the butler. "A glass of brandy?" he offered.

"Thank you, my lord," was the dazed reply. "Very kind of you."

"Now tell me what has been happening," requested Carleton, pouring himself a glass as well.

John filled him in about his trip to Brasted and what Frances had disclosed about her subsequent visit to Lady Murray. He then went on to recount what had occurred that very day when he had tried to see Frances at Devonshire Street.

"Miss Frances would never have sent me away like that, not if it were ever so. I am thinking, my lord, that perhaps Lady Murray was not so pleased to have her granddaughter prove she was legitimate as she pretended." He added shrewdly, "It seems plain to me that Miss Frances is being held there against her will."

Carleton nodded, "It would seem so! I will call on her tomorrow and see what I can discover. Where are you staying?"

"At the Regent Hotel, my lord. Miss Frances still has rooms there and some of her belongings."

"I will call on you tomorrow evening, will you be there?"

"I'll make sure of it, my lord," John replied, feeling hopeful. Lord Carleton appeared to know what he was doing.

"I am on my way to Whites, can I drop you somewhere?" Carleton asked.

"No thank you, my lord. I might take a stroll round to Devonshire Street, just to keep an eye on things."

Carleton nodded and they parted at the door. He thought he might take a leaf out of Hopgood's book, and spread the word of Frances' existence and her parents' marriage. If it became common knowledge, it would be much more difficult for Lady Murray to orchestrate a cover up. He would make an appearance at Almack's to drop the word in a few feminine ears and then call in at his club.

Entering the 'Marriage Mart,' he was fortunate enough to see Sammy Fairfax there with a party of friends, and went up to her. "Sammy, give me the next dance will you?"

"But I am already promised to Tom Humphries," she protested, smiling at him.

"Fob him off," he demanded impatiently, "I have something ex-tremely important to tell you. You will be the first person to hear the news," he offered tantalizingly.

Sammy swapped her dance with Tom in exchange for going in to supper with him, and was soon standing up with Carleton, eager to hear what he had to say.

"Do you remember the woman you met as Diana Murray?"

She nodded questioningly, her eyes fixed on his. "Yes?"

"Her real name is Frances Metcalf and she is the missing grand-daughter of Lady Anna Murray, her mother was Lady Anna's daugh-ter Amanda and her father was Henry Metcalf."

"Lud! Is it true? She said she thought she was a relation of Lady Julia Murray!" Sammy exclaimed excitedly.

"Her aunt," confirmed Carleton. "She is staying with her grand-mother at the moment. No doubt she will be presented soon."

"But how-?"

"Before you pepper me with questions, that is all I know," inter-rupted Carleton firmly. "I am sure she will have lots to tell you when you see her next. Perhaps you and your aunt might call on her one day soon," he suggested, hoping to distract her.

Despite his disclaimer, Sammy continued to plague him with unanswerable questions until he was glad to hand her off to her next partner. He stayed only to politely greet several dowagers of his acquaintance before departing for his club, before Sammy could corner him again. He took a slightly different approach to spread the tale at White's. A few simple questions as to whether George or Harry had met the latest heiress was enough to get the rumours circulating.

Unaware of the schemes being hatched on her behalf, Frances was getting tired of being compliant. She had spent a very boring day pacing her room and had even ventured to read a few pages of the improving book Lady Murray had selected for her. She had carefully explored every inch of the room, which took less than ten minutes, and had reached the conclusion that her best weapon was the chamber pot. She had spent an hour testing the strength of the bars in the window and attempting to chip away at the bricks they were embedded in, but unless she was going to be there for several weeks, the only way out was through the door.

CHAPTER 28

The following afternoon, Lord Carleton, dressed in a dark blue coat and cream pantaloons, presented himself at the door of Lady Murray's house and sent in his card. He was uncertain how he would be received but what he had not expected was to be left standing at the door and told by the butler, "I am afraid Her Ladyship is not at home. She is not receiving anyone, good day to you, my lord."

He was turning away, still bemused by the rudeness of his reception when the door opened and a small elderly woman ventured out. "I am most sorry, my lord, my mistress is a little blue-devilled at the moment. Were you wanting anything in particular? We so rarely have any gentleman callers."

Carleton stopped and looked at her, "My apologies, ma'am, I am afraid I do not remember if we have met before," he said politely.

The little woman looked flustered but answered, certain that he must be here because of Frances. "I am Mrs Pearson, my lord, I am Lady Murray's companion. I was nurse to Lady Amanda," she added.

"Ah, I see," murmured Carleton. "To be honest, I was hoping to see Miss Frances Metcalf. I understand she is staying here."

Mrs Pearson looked back nervously at the door. "I am afraid I cannot stay out here talking to you any longer, my lord, but if you should happen to be in Regent Street's lending library later this afternoon at about 4 o'clock, I might see you then."

"I shall hope to see you there," he replied and bowed his head. "Good day, ma'am."

Mrs Pearson went back inside.

"What were you doing out there?" demanded Lady Murray.

"Apologising!" she answered resolutely. "Hanson was so rude to that poor man."

Lady Murray curled her lip, "That poor man as you call him was the rake who debauched Frances!" she exclaimed crudely.

Her companion stared at her in disbelief, she could not credit it, he had been so polite, so very much the gentleman. She thought she would still go to the library later that afternoon.

Lord Carleton was inside waiting for her when she reached the library, and he came over to the same shelf she was looking at and picked up a book.

"Can you tell me what has happened?" he murmured in a low voice.

"You know that Miss Frances is her granddaughter?" she replied quietly. He nodded. "Everything was going along famously, until my lady received a report from her solicitor, Mr Pilkington, that Frances had been ... had been ..." she faltered. "It mentioned a place called Chatswood, my lord. Are you familiar with it?"

Carleton drew in his breath. "That is my home, ma'am. Let me reassure you that whatever you have heard, Frances has not done anything to be ashamed of, but, in any case ... well, the long and the short of it is I wish her to be my wife. I would marry her tomorrow if she wills it."

"Oh! My lord, I had hoped as much when you came to visit today. But my lady has taken against her and will not let anyone see her. She says she has lost her senses and has locked her in the old nursery and put a guard outside her door. I do not know what is to be done!"

"Can you meet me again tomorrow? I would think on this."

"Let me see," she thought. "I will borrow a book she has already read, then I can return it tomorrow. I will try to be here around the same time, my lord."

They separated and Carleton went off to keep his appointment with John Hopgood at the Regent Hotel. The two men took a couple of mugs of ale over to a table in a quiet corner of the taproom, and sat down while Carleton told John what had happened that afternoon. The manservant nodded, "I guessed it must be summat like that, my lord. What do you reckon we should do next?"

"We can hardly force our way into the house! At least not without creating a shocking scandal." He took a sip of ale and continued ruefully, "I confess I did consider whether one of us could break in at night and bring her out, but I doubt that would be as easy as it sounds."

John had been thinking, "This woman, the old nurse, feels kindly towards Miss Frances you say?" Carleton nodded. "Do you think she could get something to her? Her pistol mayhap? I reckon Miss Frances could get out of that house easier than we could get in."

Carleton considered the suggestion, "That's a good idea," he said. "In fact ... are her male clothes still here, in her room?" John nodded. "Then perhaps you could pack a small bag, including the pistol, and give it to Mrs Pearson. No wait, she does not know you, it would be better for you to give me the bag and I will pass it to the nurse. Then if she can get the bag to Frances, she will be able to leave the house much easier in breeches than in skirts, she could even climb out a window if necessary."

The other man was nodding in agreement, "But I don't like the idea of her coming back here," he mused. "It would be too easy for Lady Murray to swoop in with her tame doctor and whisk her off again. We will have to return to France. I will pack the rest of her belongings here, hire a post-chaise and we will be off to Dover tonight."

Carleton stared at him aghast. "Dover! I was expecting that she would come home with me!" he protested.

The other man stared at him in return.

Carleton flushed. "She will come to no harm with me. I plan to ask her to be my wife."

John was sure his mouth had dropped open. "What if Lady Murray sends the runners after her? She could say you had kidnapped her."

"I do not think so. Not even Lady Murray would wish to cause such a scandal. And in any event, she will be safe staying with me as Peter Francis."

"I do not wish to offend you, my lord," said John carefully, "but I will need to hear from Miss Frances whether she is happy to go with you or not."

Carleton nodded, "Of course. I suggest you pack up and settle the account here as you intended, but come to my house and I will put you up. I will wait for Frances tomorrow night in my carriage, then bring her home and she can decide what she would rather do. There will still be time to travel to Dover if that is her wish. If you will trust me to do so, I will write a note explaining our plan to her, and it can go in the bag with her clothes."

John agreed. "I hope this will all go as planned, my lord. If you can wait here a moment I will go and get the bag for you now." He was back in less than ten minutes with a small haversack. "Here you are, my lord. I will be around to see you tomorrow afternoon with the rest of our baggage."

Carleton took the bag, "Very good, I will tell Rawlings, my butler, to expect you. I will be at the library to meet Mrs Pearson all being well." They took their leave and Carleton went home to have his dinner and write a letter to Frances. He hoped he could persuade Mrs Pearson to deliver it to her.

Mrs Pearson had endured a half-hearted scold from Lady Murray over the twice borrowed book and allowed herself to be persuaded that she should return to the library the very next day to exchange it. Again Lord Carleton was already there when she arrived. He waited at a distance until she had dispatched the maidservant who had accompanied her on an errand, then approached her, this time as an old acquaintance for the benefit of anyone else in the library. "Mrs Pearson, I hope I find you well ma'am?" He lowered his voice, "How is she? Have you seen her?"

"Not yet," came the disappointing reply. "I will try again on my return."

"I have a small bag here containing items she may be able to use to help her escape. Do you think you might be able to get it to her?" He spoke urgently and she looked a little flustered.

"Oh, my lord, I am sure I don't know ... what does it hold?"

"Some clothes she can use as a disguise, and a letter from me," he admitted. "I know you would not normally be involved in a clandestine correspondence, but these are far from normal circumstances! You may read it if you think you must, but it is merely a letter reassuring her of my intentions," he added, hoping the last comment would dissuade her from the attempt. She blushed slightly and took the bag from him.

"I will be waiting outside tonight, in my carriage," he told her.

Feeling as if she were engaged in a thrilling adventure, Mrs Pearson said conspiratorily, "If I am not able to get the bag to her by tonight, my lord, I will leave a light on in my window, it is at the front of the house on the first floor."

"What a clever notion. You have my gratitude ma'am." He had a sudden twinge of conscience. "If per chance you should suffer from this night's work, come to me and I will help you."

They parted just before the maidservant returned from her errand. "Where ever did that bag come from, ma'am?" she exclaimed.

"I brought it to carry some library books I have borrowed for Miss Frances," the old nurse improvised. I am becoming quite good at this, she congratulated herself.

When she returned, she sought out Lady Murray straight away. "My lady, no matter what Miss Frances has done, I do think I should see her and make sure she is all right up there. I have brought some library books for her that I think will prove helpful, a book of sermons my late father was very fond of, most edifying. I am sure I shall be safe if Tom is with me," she added craftily.

Lady Murray thought for a moment. Mrs Pearson held her breath.

"Very well, Tom will take you up in a minute. Don't be upset if she appears a little.. wild, Dr Russell said the medicine she is taking has some odd side effects." In fact thought Lady Murray, I hope she becomes hysterical, it will help persuade Mrs Pearson and everyone else she is not quite right in the head and needs to be confined.

Carrying the haversack herself, Mrs Pearson followed Tom up the stairs with some trepidation. Tom opened the door without knocking and stepped inside. "You've got a visitor, Miss," he said and ushered the old nurse into the room.

"Oh, Mrs Pearson, thank heavens!" said Frances with a hitch in her voice, coming towards her. The old nurse put up a hand to fend her off. "Now there, Miss Frances," she said soothingly, "you must keep calm, you know how the doctor said any excitement is bad for you." She closed one eye, hoping Frances would take the hint. "I have brought you some books. You will find them very instructive."

She put the bag into Frances' hands, standing in front of her so that Tom could not see her face for a moment. It was just as well that she did, for Frances nearly dropped the bag in surprise, there were certainly no books inside it. Quickly she put a tremulous smile on her face, "Thank you, that is kind of you." She let a tear roll down her cheek, only half acting. "I don't like this place. Grandmother said I might go to stay in the country, do you know when?"

"No, my dear, soon I hope. I will talk to Lady Murray and see what is happening, I am sure she is doing what is best for you. I will come up and see you again tomorrow if you would like that."

"Yes please," Frances replied in a docile voice, "I am so lonely up here." She let her voice tremble and was unpleasantly surprised by how easy that was. She flung herself on the bed after the nurse left in case Tom was waiting outside to come back in and check up on her. She waited a good half hour, until her tea was brought to her, a slice of bread and butter and a glass of milk, then waited again until Tom came to clear it away, before she carefully opened the haversack. There was a note on pink writing paper on the top.

"My dear,

Tonight, when everyone is asleep, pretend to be taken ill. Call out for Tom and ask him to fetch me, then leave quickly when the door is opened. A friend awaits you in the street.

MP"

She almost burst into tears as she took out her breeches, shirt and jacket, boots for her feet and best of all her silver pistol. Wait, there was another paper folded in quarters at the bottom of the bag. She hastily drew the bed spread up to cover the clothes before unfolding the letter.

"Frances,

I love you. Come to me, I will be waiting below, all night if necessary.

Carleton"

Her heart thudded like a runaway horse while she read it again. She would wait until the house had settled for the night, and then she would go to him.

CHAPTER 29

Carleton sat fretting in silence in the dark. He had hired a hackney cab for the whole night, giving the driver ten pounds to be at his exclusive disposal. As this was more than he would make in a month, the man had been more than happy to oblige. Every so often he would flick the horse awake and they would take a turn around the block.

Impatiently, Frances waited for her dinner things to be cleared away and the household to retire for the night, then dressed thankfully in the items Mrs Pearson had brought to her. She sat down on the bed and checked that her pistol was loaded. Patience, she told herself, wait a bit longer. The minutes passed with agonising slowness until finally she heard the watchman call out the midnight hour. It was time. Hopefully Tom would have roused a little with the call.

She started groaning, gradually getting louder, "Oh my stomach," she moaned. She stumbled noisily from the bed and banged feebly at the door. "Help me, Tom, I feel so sick, I think I'm dying!"

She heard a shuffling noise, then his voice came through the door in a hoarse whisper.

"I'm not allowed to come in there, Miss. You'll be alright once you've cast up your accounts."

"It's not that, Tom, it's ..oh, I can't tell you, you would not understand. I need a female to assist me, get Mrs Pearson please, Tom!" She moaned again.

Alarmed and fearful about these mysterious feminine problems, Tom wavered for a moment then left his post in search of the old nurse, this was not something he could deal with by himself. Mrs Pearson rose quickly and draped a cloak over her nightclothes, "Whatever is the matter, Tom?" she remembered to ask.

"It's Miss Frances, she is not well. She asked me to bring you up to her," whispered Tom.

"Certainly," she agreed. "I will come straight away. Let's be careful not to wake Lady Murray," she added. Tom needed no reminder and they both crept back upstairs to the old nursery.

"Open the door, Tom," she ordered. Tom unlocked the door and opened it for Mrs Pearson to enter. His eyes went straight to the empty bed. Where was the girl?

"Come in both of you, please," came a familiar voice from against the wall, right next to the open door. Tom looked around and was dumbfounded to see a young man in front of him, pointing a pistol at him with very steady hands.

"Inside!" the youth gestured with the pistol. Mrs Pearson clung to Tom's arm, preventing him from tackling the stranger even if he had wanted to. "Oh do what she says, Tom, oh dear, I shall have a spasm for certain." She leant heavily on his arm.

Reluctantly Tom did as he was ordered, his brain only just catching up with the fact that the 'youth' wasn't a stranger at all. Tom was a strapping young man and it went against the grain for him to submit to a chit of a girl, pistol or not, but he could hardly throw Mrs Pearson to the floor.

"The key please!" demanded Frances. "I must warn you that I am a crack shot," she threatened, then added cheerfully. "Of course, I could scarcely miss from this distance!"

Tom handed the key over unwillingly. The youth, who Tom knew must be Frances, edged out of the room. "I am afraid you are not going to have a very comfortable night, but I need a head start. Give my regards to Grandmother!" Then they heard the sound of the key turning in the lock.

Tom half carried, half dragged Mrs Pearson to the bed then flung himself at the door, but as Frances had discovered previously it was exceedingly solid. Mrs Pearson sat back on the bed and looked at the ceiling, it was going to be a long night.

Frances slid noiselessly along the candlelit passage, her boots in one hand and her pistol in the other. The haversack was slung over one shoulder. She reached her blue bedroom without incident and found it much as she had left it. Hastily, she packed a few valuable items into the haversack, including her father's ring, the more costly of her wigs, the water green gown and a few small items of clothing. The rest of the articles could be retrieved later if possible, unless Lady Murray destroyed them in a fit of pique.

The front door would be locked and barred for the night. Cautiously she opened the window and leant out. Her room overlooked the front of the house and she could see the pavement about twelve feet below. She tossed her boots to the ground, swung herself out the window until she was holding on by her hands, then dropped sure footedly to the pavement.

She looked around but could see no-one waiting for her. Just then a carriage ambled quietly down the street and drew up in front of her. Carleton leant forward and opened the door, "Frances?"

"Here, my lord," she stepped into the coach without hesitating and Carleton closed the door behind her. As previously instructed, the cab picked up speed immediately, rattling over the cobblestones on its way to Carleton's house. It was dark inside the coach, Carleton wished he could see her face. "Are you all right?" he demanded.

"Nothing a bath and a good meal won't cure," she responded cheerfully. "Tell me everything that has happened! I was never so surprised to see Mrs Pearson, a conspirator! She carried everything off like an actress born!" She suddenly remembered she had left her locked in the nursery, "Oh dear, I hope she does not have too uncomfortable a night. I had to leave her and Tom prisoners in the old nursery, where they had been holding me!" she added darkly.

"Where are we going?" she asked, suddenly feeling self-conscious. She had thought from his letter that Carleton would sweep her into his arms, but perhaps he felt uncomfortable when she was dressed in men's clothes.

"My house. Your manservant Hopgood is there too," he reassured her. "He wanted you both to leave for Dover immediately but I hoped ..."

"Yes?"

"I hoped you would consider staying with me. Damn this dark! How can I tell what you are thinking if I cannot see you?"

For answer, Frances lent across the seat and kissed him on the mouth. He froze for a stunned second then pulled her roughly to him so that she was seated on his lap, his arms holding her tightly against him. He opened his mouth beneath hers and kissed her back, his tongue licking against hers, his hand caressing her down the curve of her hip and thigh. It was as if she had set a match to a powder keg. She put both arms around his neck, and wriggled around to get more comfortable.

"For heavens' sake!" he gasped, "Keep still or I shall ..I shall-"

"What?" she asked innocently.

"Never mind, I shall explain things once we are wed."

Speechless for a moment she drew back from him.

"What is the matter? Do I go too far?" He brought his hand back to her waist, peering through the darkness to try and read her expression.

"Richard, you do not have to marry me. I will be yours as long as you want me."

He swallowed. "I want you forever, Frances, marry me, please."

"Are you sure? There will be an almighty scandal, most of the ton will not recognise me you know."

"I am very sure, besides how else will I get my hands on your ten thousand pounds?" he teased.

She laughed. "In that case, yes, I will marry you, just to save you from a life of poverty."

"Kiss me again so I know you mean it," he demanded. Some breathless moments later the cab came to a halt outside Carleton's house, rather to the disappointment of both its occupants.

"Oh gad, I wish I had not told Hopgood he might stay with me, I am certain he means to act as your chaperone. I hope you are not hanging out for a long engagement, I don't think I can wait very long," he murmured as he helped her out of the carriage and paid off the driver.

"Well my parents married by special licence," said Frances demurely, "Perhaps we could do the same?"

"What an excellent idea!" They went into the house to find John Hopgood hovering anxiously in the hall. "Miss Frances, are you alright?" He came up to her, ignoring Lord Carleton for the minute.

"I am fine, John, in fact," she glanced at Carleton, "You can be the first to congratulate us, we are betrothed."

He gasped then looked sideways at the other man, "You've told him the truth? About how we have lived since you were born?"

Frances nodded and looked from one man to the other, "He knows, but so we are all clear, you may tell him again John. I have nothing to hide from him."

Hopgood looked uncomfortable, "I am sorry, Miss Frances, I did not mean to give offence, I just wanted to be sure you both know what you are about. It won't be easy, being a gamester's daughter married to a lord."

"The things most worth having in life are not always easy," Carleton agreed. A noise came from the hall behind them and they all turned as one. Fanshaw, his valet, was coming sleepily down the hallway, looking as if he had dressed hastily, "My lord?"

"Ah, Fanshaw, there you are," said Carleton smoothly. "Mr Francis has just arrived and will be staying tonight. We have some business to discuss in the study but we won't be long, I'll call you when I am ready to retire." He ushered Hopgood and Frances into the study and closed the door. "I suggest you two travel down to Chatswood tomorrow, the less we are seen here together the better I fancy. I will follow as soon as I have the Special Licence in my hand. Frances and I will be married quietly as soon as we can and then we will announce it officially and confront Lady Murray with a fait accompli."

John was nodding in agreement but Frances looked uncomfortable. "There's just one thing, Richard. Your housekeeper, Mrs Madden, wrote to Lady Murray, telling her that I stayed with you and I would prefer not to see her again if it can be avoided. It was a rather unpleasant letter."

"I feared as much!" exclaimed Carleton angrily. "I told her several times it was not her concern, however I cannot just cast her off, she has been with our family for years." He thought a moment. "I know! I will send her to Theo, I am sure Fanny, his wife, would love to have her help with the children."

"It is not just Mrs Madden, it will be an awkward situation with all your servants," commented Frances uneasily. "They will know me as Peter Francis, how will we explain that we are betrothed? I wish we could just be married straight away, and then it will not be any of their concern how I dress or how we spend our time together."

"You have the right of it I am afraid, let me think for a moment," replied Carleton.

"Tis a pity you cannot be wed at Brasted like your parents, it would be almost like a tradition. The rector seemed a good sort," observed John idly.

"Actually, that is quite a good idea!" enthused Carleton. "It is only about thirty miles from Brasted to Guildford. We could go directly to Brasted, get wed, then go on to Chatswood as a married couple. I wonder if Mrs Pearson would consent to come with us as a chaperone, and be a witness to the marriage? She was your mother's nurse so she has a history with your family and it would add an air of respectability to the affair. What do you think, Frances?"

"I think that sounds an excellent plan, Richard, I do hope she can accompany us."

"I do not think we can do anything else tonight." He glanced at the others. "I am sure we are all tired, come with me and I'll show you to your room, Frances."

"I'll just come up with you, and then I can take your boots down for a polish," said John airily and Carleton exchanged a rueful smile with Frances. They all trooped upstairs to their separate rooms, Carleton determined to be on his best behaviour in any event, whether John was hovering or not; there was going to be enough scandal as it was without the servants thinking he had spent the night with Peter Francis!

CHAPTER 30

Back in Devonshire Street, Mrs Pearson did not have such a long wait to be rescued as she had feared. Tom was a hefty young man and after a lot of ramming his shoulder against the door and even kicking it with his foot, he managed to break the lock. The old nurse tottered out behind him as he burst into the passage.

"Oh well done, Tom! I don't think we should wake Lady Murray, do you? After all, there is little to be done until morning in any case. I shall break the news to her first thing ... or perhaps after breakfast? Dear me, I wonder which would be less upsetting?"

Tom was very happy to leave the job of breaking the news to Lady Murray, to Mrs Pearson. At least her ladyship was more likely to have calmed down a little by the time she saw him.

Lady Murray was coldly furious when told the news after breakfast. "Why was I not informed of this immediately?" she demanded harshly.

"I did not want to disturb you," faltered Mrs Pearson. "What could you have done in any case? She must be half way to Dover by now."

Lady Murray stared at her with an arrested expression. "Dover? Yes, I suppose so, it is not as if she has any friends in London who would shelter her! Although I shall send Tom over to the Regent Hotel later today, just to make sure she has not gone back there. It is very aggravating, not to know where she is for certain." She turned to glare at Mrs Pearson, even though she could not actually see her. "I never thought you would be such a fool, Maria, to be taken in by her," she said coldly.

"No, my lady," murmured her companion apologetically.

The next morning, Frances, still dressed as Peter, wrote a letter for John to take to Mrs Pearson, advising her that she was going to marry Lord Carleton by special licence and asking her whether it was possible for her to accompany them on their trip to Brasted; and in addition, whether she would be able to bring all or some of her clothes with her. She added a rider to the effect that if this last was too difficult to do secretly, then not to worry herself about it. She included an invitation for her to spend a few weeks with them at Chatswood and in fact, if she liked, to leave Lady Murray entirely and stay there permanently with them.

John set off to Devonshire Street with the letter, hoping to get a chance to speak to Mrs Pearson alone. However, the butler refused him permission to enter and wait while he summoned the nurse, and John was not willing to entrust the letter to him, so they were at a standstill. He slipped around to the back of the house and hung about until eventually a maidservant came out to empty some slops. A few moments later and a shilling poorer, John was left trying to look as if he had business at the neighbouring house, while he waited for Mrs Pearson to come down to him.

She came out looking flustered and called him over speaking loudly, "I am sorry, my good man, but we do not need a coachman's services here." She bent nearer to whisper to him, "Meet me at the end of the street around four today, I will give you my answer then. Good day to you," she added in her normal voice and turned quickly back to the house. Feeling he had done all he could, John went back to Grosvenor Place.

Carleton returned to the house later that day with the special licence in his hand. He grabbed Frances round the waist and spun her about, "Not long now! Tomorrow we will be off to Brasted! Do you have anything with you to wear as a wedding gown?"

She laughed and looked hastily around to make sure they were not being observed. "I have one gown with me, that will have to do!"

John waited at the end of Devonshire Street for some time before he spotted Mrs Pearson hurrying towards him with a small carpet bag.

"Here." She said, handing it to him. "This was all I could save from Miss Frances' room. Lady Murray has given the rest to the maids or the poor house! Please tell her I cannot accompany her - I would have been very happy to see her wed, but I can think of no reason to give Lady Murray, to explain my disappearance for several days. I do not think it at all wise to tell her the truth!"

The nurse was looking anxiously over her shoulder even as she was speaking to him. "I must not tarry any longer. Please give her my heartfelt wishes for her future happiness!"

"Thank you, ma'am, I will indeed! If perchance you change your mind, we leave from Grosvenor Place tomorrow morning at ten." John bowed his head to her and strode off with the bag clutched in his hand, unaware that he was being followed.

Tom was on his way back to the house in Devonshire Street after a fruitless visit to the Regent Hotel, when he saw Mrs Pearson hand over the carpet bag to a strange man. He stopped and pretended to fiddle with the buckle on his shoe as the stranger passed him. Surely that was the manservant who had come to the house a few days ago, asking to see Miss Frances? There was something havey-cavey going on here! He decided to follow him and see where he went, he had not forgiven Frances for making a may game of him over the locked room.

Frances and Carleton were half way through their dinner when the butler came in with an affronted look on his face. "My lord, there is a person here to see you. He says he is from Bow Street!"

The two exchanged a quick look. Carleton wiped his lips with his napkin and rose to his feet. "Fiend sieze it! Couldn't he wait until after I had eaten? I wonder what business he has with me? Excuse me, Peter, I had better go and see the man."

Peter nodded and slipped quietly up to his room.

Carleton went into the hall where a stout gentleman with a red face was standing uncomfortably.

"Evenin', my lord," he offered. "We 'ave 'ad a report that a young lady wot is a bit touched in the upper works is stayin' 'ere. The complaint 'as been lodged by Lady Murray, wot is 'er legal guardian, bein' as she is not quite up to snuff, as ye might say."

Carleton's eyebrows had been rising steadily during this. "My good man, what Banbury tale is this?"

"It is my dooty to search these 'ere premises to see if this girl is 'ere or not," persisted the unhappy man.

"What girl?" asked a bewildered Carleton.

" 'er name is Frances Metcalf, my lord, she's run away!"

"Well there is certainly no one going by that name here! I give you my word on it. In fact, Rawlings?" he called the butler. "Do we have any young women staying here?"

"No, my lord." Then he added hesitantly, "Except for Amy and Ellen of course." The runner turned questioningly to him.

"Oh, the maidservants, but they have both with us for years," agreed Carleton. "I do not know Lady Murray nor why she thinks this girl is here, but I can tell you this, you have come on a fools' errand. The only guest I have is male."

The runner drew his breath, "The Lady said the girl might be a young man, my lord."

"Well which is it, a male or a female? Is the woman spinning you a Canterbury Tale? It sounds rather as if she is the one who is queer in the attic!" exclaimed Carleton

"In disguise, my lord," offered the Runner gamely.

"What is keeping you, Carleton?" came a low, world weary voice. Both men looked up to see an exquisite young gentleman descending the stairs, his short hair brushed into the latest fashion, a snowy cravat at his throat and a dark blue coat with points so high he could barely turn his chin. His right hand rested lightly on the smallsword at his side.

"Who is this fellow?" He stared at the Runner and raised a quizzing glass to his eye.

"He is from Bow Street, Peter, he seems to think you are a girl in disguise," explained Carleton, ignoring the Runner's frantic gestures of protest.

The look of offended disbelief that Frances cast on the hapless Runner, nearly overset Carleton's composure entirely.

In one smooth movement the sword was drawn and the point suddenly poised against the Runner's throat. "Would you care to repeat that to my face?" he asked silkily.

"I did not mean ... I beg pardon, a mistake ...!" stuttered the Runner, backing away. "I am sure the Lady was mistook in her convictions. I won't bother you two gentlemen anymore, good night." He practically fled out the door.

"Now, where were we?" asked Carleton leading the way back to the dining room.

"First thing tomorrow, I shall send a complaint to Bow Street," fulminated Peter, in his wake. "I don't know what sort of people they are reduced to hiring, he was obviously foxed, why else come here with such wild accusations?" The two continued to abuse the absent Runner for the benefit of the butler and the footman who were waiting on them, neither of whom noticed the amusement lurking in the back of their lord's eyes.

The next morning, Frances donned her gown and wig and turned herself back into an elegant young woman. She packed her male attire and all her other possessions into the carpet bag provided the previous day by Mrs Pearson, and waited until John and Carleton between them kept the servants occupied elsewhere so that she could slip downstairs and out to the hired carriage. The postboy holding the horses' heads paid her little attention. As she was settling herself and waiting for the others, a short elderly woman carrying a small portmanteau got out of a hackney cab and came tentatively towards the house.

"Mrs Pearson?" she called out the window. The nurse turned to her, "Oh Miss Frances, I am that glad you haven't left yet!" Her eyes were red and she was sniffing into a handkerchief.

"Please get in the carriage, ma'am," invited Frances. "Tell me, what has happened?" The elderly lady got shakily into the carriage leaving her luggage on the footpath.

"Turned off!" she said tearfully. "Me, that was with her more than forty years! I still cannot believe it. And if you cannot take me I don't know what I will do or where I will go!" She started sobbing in earnest.

"My dear lady," said Frances firmly, "Of course you will come with us, to Chatswood! Well, firstly we are going to Brasted to be wed, and then after that to Chatswood. We will be very grateful to have you I can assure you. Ah, here is John now." Hopgood came out with her luggage and stored it on the back of the coach. "Mrs Pearson is coming with us after all, John," explained Frances. "Can you put her case on the back with mine?"

"I think so, if you could take this small bag in with you, Miss," John rearranged the luggage to his satisfaction.

Carleton came out then, and greeted Mrs Pearson politely as Frances told him what had occurred. "Of course you are welcome to stay with us, ma'am," he reiterated warmly.

He had arranged for John to drive the carriage, and he had planned to ride alongside to give as much an appearance of propriety as they could, but he was very glad Mrs Pearson was coming with them and would sit inside with Frances. It would also make it possible for them all to stay overnight in Sevenoaks, if for some reason the rector was unable to perform the ceremony that day.

They set off at last, Rawlings closing the door behind them and wondering furiously who the two unknown women were, in the coach. He was staying in town to oversee the upkeep of the house in its owner's absence, and Fanshaw was to go down to Chatswood by hired chaise later that day so that he would be on hand to attend to Carleton.

Fanshaw himself, was still flabbergasted by the instructions Lord Carleton had given him that very morning.

"I am sure you will be happy to hear that I am getting wed in the next day or so to Miss Frances Metcalf, Henry Metcalf's daughter. You have not yet made her acquaintance as she has been living abroad until very recently." Lord Carleton had given him a very meaningful look at that point which he had not in the least understood.

"I need you to give these instructions to Williams, to inform the staff and prepare the household for its new mistress. And here is another letter for Mrs Madden, she will be going to live with Mr Theo's family for a while. I would greatly appreciate it if she could be taken there as soon as possible."

Although he then added a comment to the effect that Fanny had requested her help with the children, it was apparent to Fanshaw that Mrs Madden had severely angered his lordship. As she had been attached to Mr Richard and the family for years, he wondered uneasily what on earth she had done to earn his displeasure.

CHAPTER 31

B y the time they stopped for a light luncheon and change of horses at a posting house, Mrs Pearson was starting to feel more cheerful. It was a very long time since she had been anywhere without Lady Murray and she began to feel as if a weight were lifting from her shoulders. Frances told her a little about her life abroad, leaving out the more florid episodes and the nurse thought it all sounded very exciting, even if slightly shocking.

They reached Brasted as the sun came out for the first time that day, a good omen she thought. John took them straight to the rectory, and, accompanied by Lord Carleton, went up and knocked at the door. "Reverend Thomas, do you remember me? I was here a couple of weeks ago enquiring about the marriage of Henry Metcalf?"

The face in front of them cleared, "Yes of course." He looked questioningly at the fashionably dressed man beside him.

"This is my Lord Carleton, Reverend Thomas, oh and I'm Hopgood sir in case you've forgotten."

Carleton reached out to shake the reverend's hand. "How d'ye do, sir? I have an unusual request of you. May I introduce my betrothed?" At this Frances descended from the carriage and came towards the small group, followed more slowly by Mrs Pearson.

The Reverend Thomas's face lit with sudden recognition, as had Mrs Pearson previously when she first set eyes on Frances. "Henry!" he exclaimed. "I beg your pardon!" he blushed.

"No, you are correct, sir," responded Frances, smiling, "I am Frances Metcalf, Henry was my father. And this is my companion Mrs Pearson, she was also my mother Amanda's nurse."

"My goodness me! What a surprise! But how can I help you?" he inquired, puzzled.

"Miss Metcalf and I wish to be married," Carleton said firmly. "I have a special licence with me."

"But, surely, your own parish ...?" asked the rector, astonished.

Frances spoke up, "To be honest sir, we have a problem with my grandmother, Lady Murray. I have lived abroad all my life and have only just met her. You are aware from John's enquiries that she had some doubts as to whether my parents were truly married?"

The rector was nodding, "But surely I was able to put those to rest?"

"Yes indeed," responded Frances warmly, "You cannot know how grateful I am to you. But Lady Murray is reluctant to recognise me still, and I suspect there will be a legal battle over my inheritance. Lord Carleton and I wish to be married as soon as possible so that we may confront this together as husband and wife. I do not have any place to stay for the three weeks required for banns, except with my Lord Carleton, and we thought this would be a better alternative, especially since you knew my parents."

Mrs Pearson was nodding throughout this, a picture of a respectable elderly lady and the rector looked at her, "Excuse me," he glanced apologetically at Frances, "but you can confirm this?"

"Yes indeed rector, unfortunately it is all too true, my Lady's behaviour has been a grave disappointment to me and would be to her daughter too, if she were still with us, God rest her soul." She held her handkerchief to her eye again.

"I am twenty four years old, reverend, certainly of an age to know my own mind, will you do this for us? I beseech you." Frances pressed, her hands reaching out to clasp his.

More prosaically, Carleton took the licence from his pocket and handed it to the rector. "You may see everything is in order, sir."

The rector looked from one to the other and sighed. "Very well, when did you have in mind?"

"As soon as possible rector, there will be just the four of us attending. Mr Hopgood and Mrs Pearson can serve as witnesses," Carleton answered promptly.

"In that case, give me a few minutes to prepare and I will meet you over at the church."

Frances and Carleton thanked him and the small party walked the few yards to St Martin's church, pausing a few moments to admire the mullioned windows with their stone arches. In an hour or less they would be married, Frances had to pinch herself to verify that she was not asleep and dreaming, she leant over to Carleton and whispered, "Are you sure of this, Richard?"

He looked down at her, "I was never more certain of anything in my life! Not feeling missish are you?" he smiled. "Did I tell you how beautiful you look today?"

She coloured up, "You don't need to offer me Spanish coin, my lord," she scolded.

For answer, he pulled her to him and kissed her lightly on the lips, "Beautiful!" he insisted.

A few moments later, Frances Metcalf and Lord Richard Carleton were married in the same church as Frances' parents twenty five years earlier, with Mrs Pearson crying happy tears into her handkerchief and John Hopgood as witness and self-conscious groomsman, handing over the two gold rings Carleton had thoughtfully provided himself with after getting the special licence.

"Where will you go now?" asked the rector chattily after the service. "Will you travel to Chatswood this evening? I am afraid I cannot offer you any hospitality myself, but The Chequers is a fine inn at Sevenoaks, if you would prefer to stay overnight and set out tomorrow."

Carleton looked at his little party, Mrs Pearson in particular appeared rather worn and it would take at least three hours to reach Chatswood, perhaps a stay in Sevenoaks would be the best. "Thank you, reverend, I think we shall try The Chequers if that is acceptable to you Frances?"

She nodded gratefully, "I think we would all appreciate a good meal and a rest tonight, Richard."

They thanked Reverend Thomas again and John drove them to Sevenoaks, where they soon found The Chequers to be as warm and inviting as the rector had promised, particularly when John announced they were newlywed. Carleton and Frances were shown the best room and promised a small parlour where they could eat their dinner in private. Mrs Pearson said a tray in her room would suit her best and John decided he would eat in the common room so that the couple could have their first meal as man and wife by themselves.

Frances looked at Carleton a little shyly as they sat down to their dinner, "I think this is the first time we have been alone that I have not been dressed as Peter."

He laughed, "Perhaps when we are at home, you can dress as Peter sometimes for old times' sake, if you would like to, that is?"

She looked at him in pleased surprise, "Yes, I would like that, if you do not think our neighbours would be too shocked. Especially for riding," she added darkly, "I never liked riding with a side saddle, one always feels about to fall off! You do not mind seeing me in breeches?"

He lowered his voice, "I love seeing you in breeches, you have beautiful long legs. Perhaps you will start a new fashion." Frances flushed again and Carleton lost all interest in food. He leant across the table and said, "I can hardly wait to make love to you but I will not rush you, any time you feel uncomfortable, just tell me to stop and I will."

"You make me fall in love with you all over again when you say things like that," she told him, smiling into his eyes. "I think I have eaten sufficient, what about you?"

He was on his feet and around the table almost before she had finished speaking, "Let's go to our room, now!" His voice was hoarse, as he drew back her chair and ushered her out of the parlour. As soon as he had shut the bedroom door they were in each others' arms, kissing frantically, Carleton holding her tightly against him. Eventually he wrenched his mouth away and put his hands unsteadily on her shoulders, "Do you need help to take off your dress?"

He tried to calm himself enough so that he could undo the tiny buttons without ripping them off, that would hardly reassure her he would be a gentle lover, nor did Frances have that many spare clothes to trifle with! Finally he managed to undo enough buttons so that she could take the gown off herself, and he hastily pulled off his boots and stripped off his clothes as fast as he could.

By the time he was naked, she had slipped under the bed covers and was watching him wide-eyed. He slid in next to her and gently drew her towards him. The feel of her smooth skin against his side was nearly enough to drive him wild again, "We will take this slowly," he whispered, lightly stroking her hair, "Let's lie here and get accustomed to the feel of each other. Kiss me, Frances."

She leant closer and kissed his mouth, her breasts pressing against his side, she loved the warm feel of his arm around her and his hand on her back and pressed harder against him. His other hand came around to caress the curve of her hip, then up to her breasts. She reached out to tentatively run her hand over the hard muscles of his chest then slowly explored lower down to his flat stomach. "Tell me what to do."

CHAPTER 32

Morning sunlight shining in the window woke Frances to find herself spooned against her husband, his arm resting lightly across her breast. She turned to cuddle into him and looked into delighted brown eyes already widening in arousal, "Good morning, wife," he said, before kissing her. "How do you feel this morning?"

"Hungry!" came the prosaic answer. He laughed and was about to get reluctantly out of bed, when she pulled him back down with a teasing smile, "Hungry for you, my lord."

"I love it when you call me that," he groaned, taking her in his arms again. They were very late downstairs for breakfast that morning but no-one seemed surprised!

Their two servants and companions had already eaten and were packing their bags, and John offered to help Carleton with his boots if he wished it. Frances dressed herself in a sprigged muslin gown that Mrs Pearson had salvaged from her room at Lady Murray's; once settled at Chatswood, she would require the urgent services of a dress maker, for the second time in as many weeks. In a short time the party was on their way again, this time to Chatswood, Carleton riding again to give the ladies more space in the carriage. He hoped Fanshaw had already taken Mrs Madden to Theo.

The afternoon sun was glinting on the windows of Chatswood when they arrived, Williams braced on the steps at the front to greet them, a polite, if rather fixed, smile on his face. What bumble-broth had his lord got himself into this time? He was reassured to see Mrs Pearson's respectable figure descend from the carriage, and looked past her with an unexpected degree of optimism that his new mistress would not be too far beneath his master's touch. His first impression was hopeful, the young woman now descending was elegant and graceful and then he caught a good look at her face.

He froze. Surely that wasn't? No of course it could not be, a chance resemblance only. He gathered himself together as Carleton came towards him, his wife's hand on his arm. "Frances, this is Williams, Williams my wife Lady Frances, and her companion Mrs Pearson. I am sure you will serve my wife as well as you have served me."

"Welcome, my lady," he murmured, still staring after her as they all went into the house. He had almost convinced himself the resemblance was less strong than he had thought, when he caught sight of Fanshaw, who was waiting to greet his new mistress. He looked like nothing more than a stuffed pike, his mouth was even gaping open slightly. "Ah, Fanshaw," Carleton greeted him smoothly, "Let me present my wife to you, as I said earlier, she has recently come from abroad."

Fanshaw looked blankly at his master for a moment before understanding dawned on him. He gulped. "Of course, my lord." He looked at Frances and blushed involuntarily, "Welcome ... er ... my lady," he managed.

Carleton frowned at him but Frances drew him away to introduce her to the rest of the staff before he could say anything. "Richard, you will need to give them time to grow accustomed to me," she said quietly.

"I will dismiss anyone who is insolent to you!" He said angrily under his breath.

"Very well, but let's make allowances for a few days; you must admit it is quite a shock. Thank goodness we have Mrs Pearson with us to lend us some respectability!" She added with a wry smile.

The next few days went better than Frances had expected. There were numerous sideways looks when they thought she was unaware, but none of the servants were openly hostile to her as Mrs Madden had been. She thought the real test for Richard would be in his relationship with the squire. If Squire Herbert gave either of them the direct cut, not only would it bring home to Carleton that he was now on the outskirts of society, but it would be very uncomfortable for the whole neighbourhood, forcing the local people to take sides.

She remembered the squire had been a blunt man, who she thought would appreciate an honest approach. She suggested to Richard that they invite the Squire to call on them one morning by himself to discuss an item of business, so that he did not have to make an immediate decision as to whether he would recognise the new Lady Carleton socially or to bring his family with him.

"After your business is concluded, you may introduce me and I shall tell him a little of our story, then it will be up to him whether he chooses to be our friend or not."

Carleton agreed this was a sensible idea and sent off a messenger requesting the squire to call on him in the next day or so.

When Squire Herbert had heard the news that there was a mistress at Chatswood he had been thrown into disarray. Was it the French girl he had met a few weeks ago or not? He was relieved to get the message from Carleton asking him to call, now he could go and see for himself, he hoped Carleton had not been gulled by a bit of muslin.

He presented himself the next day and his heart sank when he recognised the woman with Richard. However he was pleasantly surprised by her modest appearance and graceful manners as she invited him to be seated and take some refreshment while she explained her situation in perfect English.

"Richard and I thought we should explain a little of our circumstances to you, Squire. Your suspicions are correct, I was here before, masquerading as Peter Francis. I had recently arrived in England from abroad and was trying to establish my identity of which there was some question. I now know that my real name was Frances Metcalf and my parents were from Sevenoaks in Kent, my mother was Lady Amanda Murray and my father her second cousin, Henry Metcalf."

Squire Herbert was listening, eyes wide.

"My grandmother is Lady Anna Murray and she is attempting to deny my claim to my mother's estate, which is the sum of ten thousand pounds!" At this he glanced in amazement at Richard for confirmation and saw him nodding his head. "Now Richard and I are married, he will be able to confront my grandmother and insist on my inheritance. I would not marry him until I was certain I was legitimate," she confessed, giving a reason he could understand for the masquerade.

"Upon my word that sounds an astonishing tale!" exclaimed the Squire candidly, not meaning any insult.

Frances nodded in agreement, leaning forward, "Yes indeed, I would scarcely believe it myself, if it had not happened to me! Mrs Pearson, who is staying with us, has letters from my parents announcing my birth. She is my mother's old nurse and was companion to my grandmother before coming to me," she explained. "My parents' marriage is recorded in the parish register at St Martin's in Brasted."

"I realise our earlier conduct must seem rather ... unconventional," Carleton ventured earnestly, "But I can assure you-" He broke off as the Squire hastily put out a hand to stop him, "Not my business!" he said quickly, going slightly red in the face. "No need to explain anything to me, Carleton."

"Very well," conceded the other man. He did not want to put the Squire on the spot, but he also wished to start as he meant to go on, to let people know that he and his wife would not be shunning society. "Frances and I will hold a dinner party in a couple of weeks to introduce her to our local society, I do hope you and Marianne will be free to attend, but I will send an invitation once we are more settled."

Will Herbert murmured something non-committal and took his leave of them both politely.

"I think that went well, for the most part," offered Frances.

Carleton was frowning, still uncertain whether he should have insisted on telling the Squire he had not laid a hand on Frances until after they were wed. Frances stepped close to him and whispered in his ear, "Don't let it worry you, no one with eyes in their head is going to believe I didn't have my way with you as soon as I had the chance."

Carleton gave a startled laugh, then kissed her, "Now that you mention it, perhaps you could have your way with me again," he said suggestively.

Lady Murray was fuming. Her plan to control Frances had gone terribly astray, and not only that, but she had been forced to dismiss Mrs Pearson, her sole companion for the last twenty five years.

Mr Pilkington, standing gravely before her, had been unable to offer any real solution to her difficulties. "There is little we can do, my lady," he told her, with a long face. "Lord Carleton is obviously prepared to put her under his protection, and if he marries her as Mrs Pearson seemed to think, she will be quite beyond our reach. I assume there is no possibility of a reconciliation between the two of you?"

She snorted, "Over my dead body!"

"In that case, the only advice I can give you is to continue to deny her claims and stretch the settlement of the inheritance out as long as you can."

Lady Murray dismissed him and sat considering, there must be something else she could do.

Unbeknownst to her, the Comte Duverne was scheming along similar lines. After his unsuccessful attempt to injure the youth he had known as Louis Caron, he had sent his manservant to the

Pelican the following day to find out what was happening and he had been regaled with a highly coloured account of the attack and the subsequent departure of 'Peter Francis' to somewhere in the country. 'Peter Francis' had then dropped out of sight.

The Comte had other business to occupy him in London, but his desire for revenge kept simmering in the background. He did not fully understand why he had taken such insult at this particular incident but there was something about the boy that aggravated him intensely. He remembered the name of the man the boy had accompanied to the opera, and kept an occasional eye on his comings and goings. Eventually his patience paid off, and his informant had seen Lord Carleton leaving for his country estate with the boy's servant driving his coach, surely the boy must be somewhere at hand.

A few days later he followed discreetly and took rooms in nearby Guildford, declaring that he was seeking to buy a small property in the area. He sent his manservant out daily to observe Carleton and his household, with orders to report back immediately if he caught sight of a young man in his company. He was just starting to attract unwanted attention for his lengthy stay in the neighbourhood, when his servant reported he had seen a young man out riding with Carleton that very morning on their way to the village. The Comte dressed in his plainest clothes and rode off to Chatswood himself, leaving his servant at the inn, he wanted no witnesses to his revenge.

He had familiarised himself with the locality the first day he had arrived in the area, and lost no time in making his way to the woods overlooking the pathway between Chatswood and Selby. If only they had not already returned! His hopes were based on the supposition that the two men would have stopped and spent some time on errands or business in the village. He tethered his horse out of sight and then walked until he found a vantage point where he could see a good way down the path, but stay unseen himself behind the hedgerows. He checked his pistol and waited impatiently.

Frances had ventured forth for the first time, dressed in Peter's clothes, accompanied by Carleton to pay a visit to the village, she considered it time to live up to her growing reputation as an Original. Unsurprisingly, she had received a mixed reception, although once the word got around that she had lived most of her life abroad, many just shrugged knowingly. That would explain it! They would wait and see how she conducted herself, before making up their minds about her. The fact that she was happy to put in a standing order for both food and household items from the village shop keepers was a point in her favour. It seemed like her new Ladyship was a right 'un, not too high in the instep to buy honest local goods instead of sending to London.

They were returning home, well content with the expedition, letting the horses amble along as they chatted to each other, when Carleton, who was looking ahead to see how much further they had to go, caught sight of a gun muzzle protruding from the bushes and flung himself towards Frances shouting, "Look out!"

Almost simultaneously there was a loud report. Carleton slumped against her, a patch of red blossoming on his shoulder, as Frances grabbed hold of him with her left arm and drew her pistol in one fast motion with her right. She brought it up in an automatic reflex and fired at the spot where the shooter had been hiding in less than a second.

CHAPTER 33

"Richard! Are you alright?" She knew it was a foolish question as soon as the words left her lips, he had swooned against her, blood running down his arm. Her first instinct was to keep riding in case there were any more assailants, but then she realised she would have to stop and attend to the bleeding first. She slid hastily off her horse, trying to hang on to Richard and break his fall to the ground. She laid him on his back and pulled open his coat and shirt; it looked as if the bullet was still lodged in his shoulder and although she didn't think it was near any vital organs, it was bleeding profusely.

She loosened her own clothes, drew out the piece of cloth she had used to bind her breasts and used it to make a pad for the wound. Then for the first time, she drew breath and looked around. The two horses were still standing obediently where she had left them. She tied Diablo's reins around his neck so he wouldn't trip and gave him a slap on the rump to send him trotting off home. Then she did the same with her roan. That should bring help faster than anything else she could think of.

She had heard nothing apart from Richard's slow breathing and the pounding of her own heart since the shot, she could only hope that either she had hit the assailant or he had fled. She was not about to leave Richard and go and see. Now that the action was over, her whole body began to shake and she sat down in the dirt and put Richard's head on her lap, who on earth would want to kill him? Where was John when she needed him?

John Hopgood was outside the stables blowing a cloud with Toby, Carleton's groom, when the two riderless horses trotted in to the stable yard, and knew instantly that something was badly wrong.

"I'll take the roan back along the path. Toby, you get the gig out and follow me in case one of them is badly injured," he ordered, leaping into the saddle as he spoke. Not waiting to see if Toby was obeying, he galloped down the path to the village, his heart in his mouth. He had a moment of guilty relief, ruthlessly suppressed, when he saw that it was Lord Carleton on the ground and not Frances.

"He's been shot!" called out Frances, "Someone shot at us from those bushes!" Hopgood felt his jaw drop. Hastily he dismounted and went to check on Carleton, saw that Frances was shaking and spoke soothingly.

"He'll be fine, everything will be alright, you'll see. Toby is coming with the gig," he advised, expertly running his hands over the bandage. "You've done a good job with this. When Toby gets here, I'll drive the gig back with you and send him to fetch the doctor, he'll find him faster than I would. I am just going over to have a look behind the hedgerow, see if I can find anything to show us who did this. You'll be right?"

Frances nodded and John left her to investigate. He peered cautiously behind the hedge and gasped audibly. There was a dead man on the ground, at least, he bent over and took a closer look, yes that was definitely a bullet hole, right in the middle of his chest and his eyes were wide open, staring at the sky. What was more he knew him. It was the Comte Duverne. So the chances were very high that Carleton had taken the bullet meant for Frances. Slowly he stood up and walked back to them.

Frances looked at him questioningly.

"It was the Comte," John told her reluctantly. "You shot him?"

"Yes," replied Frances, "At least, I fired at the place the shot came from. Did I hit him then?"

"Well, not to make a meal of it, you hit him right in the chest. Killed him stone dead!" Hopgood waited rather uneasily for her reaction. It was not quite what he had expected.

"Good!" said Frances rather savagely. "That will teach him to shoot Richard!"

"We'll have to report this to the authorities. Who is the local magistrate do you know?"

"Squire Herbert, I imagine," she answered after a moment's thought.

They both froze at the sound of a horse coming towards them but it was merely Toby with the gig.

"I don't think you should tell anyone how you met the Comte in France," suggested John in a low voice before Toby should overhear them, "Let everyone think he was after Lord Carleton."

She nodded and climbed into the gig. The two servants lifted Carleton, mercifully still unconscious, up into her arms and John sent Toby off to find the doctor and the Squire. He drove as carefully as he could back to the house, but his passengers were still jolted uncomfortably, and Frances was vastly relieved when at last they drew up in front of the steps. Fanshaw and Williams were both there already, waiting anxiously. Fanshaw jumped towards them but the elderly butler paled as he saw his master sprawled in the gig, his jaw working.

"It's all right, he is not dead, just wounded," reassured Frances hastily. "He needs your aid," she added, rightly guessing this would best help them regain their composure. Fanshaw came forward to help John lift Carleton out of the gig and carry him into the house. Williams went ahead to organise the other servants into fetching Mrs Pearson, along with hot water and old sheets for bandages, then led the rescue party into the front parlour, where they laid their master on a couch.

"Toby has gone for the doctor," Frances told the group of worried servants gathered around, while carefully checking that her bandage was still in place. "I don't think we can do any more until he has seen him, I don't want to start the bleeding again by trying to clean the wound."

"What happened, my lady?" asked Fanshaw in alarm.

"He was shot. A man was hiding in the hedgerow and waylaid us as we rode by," was the calm answer.

"Shot! A poacher?" queried a horrified Fanshaw.

"I do not think so, it seems hardly likely a poacher would mistake us for game. It is not as if we were in the forest either, we were riding on a public road, he must have seen us quite clearly before firing." Frances replied thoughtfully. "Toby has gone to ask Squire Herbert if he can come and look into this. There is the matter of the body, too, that will need to be removed."

"Body?" gasped the butler.

"I am a good shot," replied Frances in a satisfied voice, oblivious of the various looks of horrified respect cast upon her.

"Oh well done, my lady!" enthused Fanshaw. He, for one, had no doubts this had been the right thing to do, any misgivings he had felt that she had gulled his lordship into the marriage were swept away instantly.

Mrs Pearson arrived then from the dairy, where she had been watching the maid churn butter, and soon had the staff dispatched about their business while Frances told her what had occurred.

I hope Lady Murray did not have a hand in this, the thought popped into her head, unspoken.

A short time later the doctor bustled into the room, ushered in by Williams. "Gunshot is it?" he asked, "My word, what is the world coming to?"

In a few moments he had everyone out apart from Fanshaw to hold down the patient in case he woke, and Frances to assist him while he extracted the bullet. "Ah, there it is!" he said triumphantly, and soon had the wound cleaned and bandaged. "Now keep him still and quiet for a few days, no wine or heavy food, and he should be as right as a trivet in no time." Squire Herbert came in silently as he was speaking, and stood watching, holding back his questions until the doctor had finished.

"Ah, a sorry business, Squire, when a man cannot even ride safely in broad daylight!" The doctor exclaimed, packing up his bag. "Lord Carleton has a bullet wound to the left shoulder. He is very lucky it was not any lower, but as it is, it should not cause him too much trouble, as long as he is careful while it heals. Well unless you have any questions for me, I will be off."

Williams escorted the doctor out, while Frances invited the Squire to be seated. He sat down reluctantly, made a little uncomfortable by the fact that she was in breeches and kept his eyes on her face. "What can you tell me, Lady Carleton?"

CHAPTER 34

"I am certain you wish to be off to examine the scene, so I will not keep you long. Richard and I were riding back along the public path from Selby, when someone shot at him from the hedgerows. I fired back immediately and John tells me I hit the man and killed him." Frances summarised succinctly.

"Did you see anything suspicious beforehand?" he enquired, taking this in his stride.

"No, nothing ... but Richard may have. I remember he called out a warning to me just before he was shot."

"And the assailant? Do you have any idea who he was?"

"I never saw him," she replied honestly. "I stayed with Richard. It was John, my manservant, who went to investigate when he arrived to help us; but I can tell you one more thing," she paused briefly, "I am certain it was no accident! Well, you will see for yourself, Squire. If you do not mind, I will stay here. John will take you to the body if that is agreeable to you?"

Squire Herbert acquiesced, and Hopgood was sent for to accompany him back to the scene of the crime. They rode the couple of miles, John slowing as they neared the scene. "It was about here," said John dismounting. "Look there is some blood on the road, that must be where Lord Carleton was lying." He turned back the way they had come, "The body ought to be over there. Would you like me to show you, sir?"

"No I'd better look for myself, if you wouldn't mind waiting here, Hopgood?"

The Squire spent a few moments looking up and down the path first, then walked slowly to the hedgerow and soon saw the body of a man, lying where he had fallen on the ground. He bent down to examine the body. The cause of death was obvious, a bullet to the chest. Gingerly he reached into the man's coat pockets and drew out about ten shillings, a couple of French coins, a linen handkerchief and the stub of a coach ticket to Guildford.

Interesting. It was clear the man was not a local, in fact the indications were he was not even English. Squire Herbert stood up and looked around in the immediate vicinity of the body and soon spotted a pistol in the grass to his right. He picked it up and sniffed it, yes, it had definitely been fired recently. He judged where the assailant would have been standing when he was shot and peered through the hedgerow to ascertain what he would have seen. He found himself in agreement with Lady Carleton, it had undoubtedly been a deliberate ambush.

"I doubt that there is anymore to learn here. Would you wait here to guard the corpse and I shall send some of my men to collect it and take it to the church," Squire Herbert requested. John nodded in resignation and sat down to wait.

The squire was already thinking ahead, he would need to send a man to Guildford to canvas the inns for a missing guest. Once they knew the identity of the assailant, it might give them a lead to the motive. When Lord Carleton regained his senses he would ask him to have a look at the corpse and see if he recognised him, but the more he considered it, the more he fancied the man was a foreigner. French possibly, if the coins in his pocket were an indication.

At least, from what he had seen so far, there was no doubt the man had been killed in self-defence. He could not quite believe Lady Carleton had shot him herself, and suspected it had actually been her husband who had fired the gun, although how he had managed it with a wounded shoulder was something to mull on.

Carleton came to his senses gradually and discovered that his shoulder hurt like the devil and he was lying on the couch in the front parlour. What on earth had happened? Frances saw that he was awake and hastened to his side. Gently she kissed his forehead, "How do you feel? You saved my life, you realise?"

"What?" he asked, still half in a daze.

"You were shot, do you remember?"

She saw he was struggling to recollect what had occurred and filled him in. "I fired back, in the direction of where I thought the shot had come from, and I hit him. To be more precise, John says I killed him. It was the Comte Duverne. Richard, I am so sorry, it is all my fault you were shot!"

"Nonsense!" was the firm reply. "What ailed the man to think he could get away with murder? He must have had windmills in his head! Did you send for Squire Herbert?"

She nodded, "John has taken him to the scene just now."

"I suggest you keep mum about your previous encounter with Duverne, though," Carleton recommended, holding her gaze.

"Yes, John advised the same, but I have been able to tell the truth so far about the shooting because it is quite true that I did not see a thing!" agreed Frances. She glanced down at her shirt, still spattered with Richard's blood. "I need to go upstairs and change my clothes. I'll just ask Fanshaw to stay with you until I return, in case you need anything. You must not try and do anything for yourself for a day or so the doctor ordered."

The next day, Squire Herbert found Lord Carleton had been removed upstairs to his bed, but he was awake and waiting to talk to him, and after a brief exchange of greetings, he was ready to answer the Squire's questions. "The only thing I saw, Will, was the gun muzzle pointing towards us. I shouted a warning to Frances, then I was hit and I don't remember anything else until I came to my senses in the front parlour. Have you found out anything about the man yet? Was he a footpad?"

"Unlikely I think, for one thing he was too well dressed to be a footpad, his coat was made by Weston and his hands were those of a gentleman, white and well cared for. He may even be someone known to you. I suspect he may have been French, or recently come from France, for he had French coins in his pockets."

"A spy?" interjected Carleton.

Squire Herbert frowned. "I had not thought of that, but what would a spy be doing here? And why lay in ambush for you? No, I do not think it. I will do my best to describe him to you, betwixt thirty and forty years, medium height I would say, black hair, olive complexion but no distinguishing features apart from that. Does that sound familiar at all?"

Carleton shook his head, "Certainly not anyone I know closely. A passing acquaintance? Possibly."

"I wish you were able to take a look at him! He will have to be buried soon, we can't keep him much longer, even in the crypt," the Squire fretted.

"Perhaps, if I were well bandaged, I could manage the journey in my carriage," Carleton pondered aloud. He had to tread carefully here, if he had not already known the identity of his assailant he would certainly have been anxious to find out everything that he could about him. He could not afford to appear too complacent.

The Squire brightened at that. "That would be excellent, if you could manage it without re-opening your wound," he felt obliged to add. "I sent a man to Guildford this morning to check if our man was staying at one of the inns, but apart from that, there is not much else I can do at present. I shall take my leave of you now and hope to see you this afternoon at the church. If you can get there, my men can carry the body out to the carriage for you to cast your eyes over."

"I shall do my best," promised Carleton.

"Oh, just one thing," remembered the Squire. "Lady Carleton told me it was she who shot the man?" he said enquiringly.

"Yes indeed, if she said so," confirmed Carleton. "Frances is an excellent shot, I have seen her at target practice myself! Just ask her to show you if you would like proof."

In spite of Frances' misgivings and indeed his own weariness, Carleton insisted on making the trip to the village church, protected with cushions as well as he could be against the jolting of the carriage.

Frances reluctantly stayed behind so that she would not risk being asked to view the body, she was trying hard to avoid lying outright to the Squire. Squire Herbert was waiting at the church, having been informed by Toby of Carleton's imminent arrival, and he quickly ordered two of the village men to bring the body out from the crypt to the carriage on a litter as he had promised.

One of the men lifted the sheet covering the body so Carleton could see the face and he looked carefully at it before shaking his head. "I don't know him, though he does have rather the look of a Frenchman I have seen around town, but he is a count, the Comte Duverne, I think he is called. This fellow is unlikely to be him!"

"Astonishing as it may seem, I have reason to believe this is in fact the Comte Duverne. There was certainly a man of that name staying at the King and Crown in Guildford who is now missing. You weren't acquainted with him at all?" the Squire looked puzzled.

"No, I've never spoken a word to him!" said Carleton honestly. "I cannot imagine what I have done to warrant such a deed. Surely if I had offended him in some way, he would have confronted me openly, as one gentleman to another, not hidden in ambush like a common footpad!"

"It's beyond belief!" agreed the magistrate. "Perhaps he mistook you for someone else?"

"It's a mystery. Either he was queer in the attic or else I deeply offended him in some way without even being aware of it! Do you think to contact the French embassy about the matter?"

"I suppose I must," the Squire agreed reluctantly. "I had best ride up to London myself and see what I can discover, he may have family there who would wish to make arrangements about the burial. At least there is no doubt about what took place. Thank you again for coming here." The Squire bowed his head and gestured to the men to return the body to the crypt. Carleton returned home slowly, grateful to get back into bed despite himself.

The Squire's trip to the French embassy, although enlightening, produced no information to explain the attack. In fact the man he spoke to was quick to distance himself from the Comte, stating emphatically several times that he was not connected to the embassy and was barely known to them. It was soon apparent to Will Herbert that the late Comte had not been a popular man.

His visit to Bow Street bore more fruit. Lord Carleton's name was familiar to the man he explained his situation to, and he sent someone in search of the Runner involved in the affair. Mr Higgins was at first reluctant to speak to anyone involved with Lord Carleton, he still felt his pulse leap unpleasantly when he remembered the feel of the sword point against his throat, but when it was explained to him that Carleton was currently laid up in the country with a gunshot wound, he was able to come forward and speak more or less sensibly to the Squire.

"I never heard anything about no Count," he shook his head dubiously. "It were a Lady wot sent me there, Lady Murray 'er name was. She was dead set to get 'er 'ands on a girl she reckoned had run away from 'er. Frances Metcalf, that was 'er name, very keen to get 'er back she was. Dunno why she thought this Lord Carleton had 'er, but I went there to ask 'im and ended up in the suds over it. Girl weren't there o'course. Just this this young'un, looked like 'e 'ad 'is mother's milk on 'is lips, but 'e had his sword at my throat quick as a flash. Right bumble-broth it was. I reckoned it was the old Lady wot was dicked in the nob, not any missin' girl."

Squire Herbert, readily identifying the presence of Peter Francis in this story, clarified a few details then thanked the Runner for his help and set out on the return journey. So far the only person who appeared to have a grudge against Lord or Lady Carleton was this Lady Murray, who, he remembered, was Frances' grandmother.

He wondered whether it was possible that, having failed with the Runners, Lady Murray had somehow engaged the Comte Duverne to take care of her problem for her in a more permanent manner. However, it seemed unlikely he would find sufficient evidence of this to warrant approaching her about it. Hopefully the Comte's violent end would put paid to any further schemes.

CHAPTER 35

A fortnight later, Lord Carleton had recovered sufficiently from his injury and they decided it was time to return to London and re-enter society. Fanshaw, Hopgood and Mrs Pearson all went with them.

Carleton's first step was to contact Mr Adams, his solicitor and brief him about Frances' claim for recognition of her birth and inheritance. He also put him in possession of the letters retrieved by Mrs Pearson concerning Frances' history, and the record of her parents' marriage. Mr Adams left them with a sombre look on his face and a cautious warning about not getting their hopes up, but secretly feeling rather thrilled by the most exciting case he had ever been presented with.

The couple's next step was to send invitations to a carefully selected group of friends for a dinner party at their house at the end of the month. Jack Lambert, Harry Belmont and Sammy Fairfax were among the small guest list, along with cousin Theo and his wife Fanny. "Might as well face everybody at once!" ventured Frances, bravely.

Carleton agreed, "Yes, it is best to know where we are placed as soon as possible. If these people will stand our friends, we should brush through tolerably well, no-one else apart from Lady Murray will be in a position to cause trouble."

Several days later, Mr Pilkington called on Lady Murray, his normally sober face even more dour than usual. He was shown in to the front parlour, where his client was seated in front of the small fire which was kept burning most of the year apart from high summer. She wore a deep blue morning dress, its high neck buttoned up to her chin and a white cap on her head. A book lay face down on the small table beside her, indicating that Annie had been reading to her prior to his arrival. She looked up at him with a slight frown. "You have news for me?" she enquired.

"Yes, my Lady. I had a visit from Mr Adams yesterday, he is Lord Carleton's solicitor," he explained. Her hand clenched briefly on the arm of her chair. "What does he have to do with this business?"

"I am afraid matters are now serious, perhaps I should say more serious," he paused for an instant then took the plunge. "They are married, Lady Murray. Miss Frances is now Lady Carleton and they are here in London. She is being introduced to the ton, not only as Lord Carleton's new wife but as your granddaughter."

"How dare she!" Lady Murray hissed incredulously.

"I am sorry, my lady, but Mr Adams showed me copies of several letters supporting her claim, letters about her birth from Lady Amanda and her father Henry Metcalf, addressed to her aunt Lady Julia. I really do not consider there is any doubt of her pedigree."

He let her digest the unwelcome news for a moment, then continued carefully. "Mr Adams presented me with an offer from

Lord Carleton on behalf of his wife, that he requested me to present to you."

Mr Pilkington cleared his throat and attempted to infuse a positive tone to his voice, really it was a very generous offer though he doubted Lady Murray would see it that way. "In return for your public acceptance of Frances Carleton as your legitimate granddaughter, they will forgo any request for distribution of her inheritance until you ..uh..well, until you pass on and the estate is wound up."

"Over my dead body!" The words burst forth uncontrollably. "I'll not have that ... that strumpet in my house again!" Two red spots flared in her cheeks.

Mr Pilkington persevered, "There is no request for a private relationship or a reconciliation, merely your public acceptance of the facts. My lady, please think of the scandal if you should challenge her claim, your families' intimate correspondence paraded before all, the subject of common gossip! And I do not need to remind you of the difficulties we would face if we are directed to pay out the money now! I strongly suggest you give this your deepest consideration, I will leave you to think about it and call again tomorrow, if it please you." He bowed himself out as he spoke, anxious to leave before she could cut loose in earnest.

Lady Murray snapped her fan in two and threw it in the fire. Fiend seize it! Mrs Pearson had betrayed her, it appeared that Henry's brat had won.

It was pouring with rain when Mr Adams called on Lord and Lady Carleton a few days later, Frances hoped it was not an omen. The solicitor came straight to the point. "I have heard from Mr Pilkington. Lady Murray has decided to accept your offer, reluctantly I understand, but at least you will not have to suffer a public brangle; she has agreed not to impugn your right to be recognised as Frances Metcalf and her granddaughter."

"Thank goodness!" exclaimed Frances.

"I admit, this has given me some concerns about the substance of your inheritance," added Mr Adams with pursed lips.

"You suspect it has been spent already?" queried Carleton, his brows raised.

"I fear so, my Lord. I do not wish to give offence, but I fear only the most powerful necessity would have compelled Lady Murray to acknowledge your wife." He bowed his head respectfully towards Frances.

"Still, we have her agreement, which is more important to me at the moment," declared Frances. "We can wait for the money."

"I shall keep a close eye on Mr Pilkington and his affairs," continued Mr Adams with relish, "Let him know he is being watched and cannot expect to get away with anything underhand in the future."

The dinner party had been arranged for that very night. Carleton had invited Theo and Fanny to arrive a little earlier than the rest of the guests as he thought they deserved to be introduced to Frances and told the story first. Remembering Theo's reaction to the part of the story he was already aware of, Carleton could only hope they would not turn around and walk out.

In fact Theo had wondered long and hard whether to accept Richard's invitation or not. He had been absolutely stunned to hear that Richard was married. In the light of what he had discovered at Chatswood, he could only assume Richard had found his missing 'friend' and married her. In the end, it was his wife Fanny who had persuaded him that they should go.

"You must trust Richard," she urged. "He is no green boy to fling his hat over the windmill, you must trust that he would not have married someone totally unacceptable. He is family, Theo; whatever the outcome, we must stand by him, even if she is not ... not good ton; in any event, we must make the best of it. You know you would hate it if you became seriously estranged from him. He will find it hard enough I suspect to steer a smooth path through Society, without his family taking against her."

"You are right, my love," agreed Theo, steadfastly pushing to the back of his mind all the spiteful things Mrs Madden had poured into his unwilling ears.

They paused at the entrance to Carleton's house, unconsciously bracing themselves and trod up the steps determined to put a brave face on things. Lord Carleton greeted them with a relieved smile as they entered the hall, "Theo, Fanny, I am so glad to see you!" but before he could introduce Frances, Theo stepped up to him to enquire anxiously about his shoulder. Carleton had written to them about the shooting incident when he had recovered sufficiently to hold a pen.

"How are you, Richard? I was never so shocked, attacked in broad daylight!" exclaimed Theo.

"I am quite recovered, as you see," replied his cousin. "I was lucky, it was but a flesh wound. Let me introduce you to my wife, Frances." He drew forward the young woman standing at his side as he spoke. Fanny saw an elegant woman, taller than herself, dressed in a pale blue silk gown which was the height of fashion, with fair hair gathered in ringlets at the top of her head and grey eyes that smiled hesitantly at her.

"I am pleased to meet you both," she said in a low, clear voice. "Will you come into the drawing room? Richard and I have a lot to tell you!"

Feeling slightly reassured by her refined manner, whoever Frances was, she was certainly no prime article, the Talbots took a seat in the drawing room and prepared to listen. Frances told them only a little about her life with her father, before moving on to describe in detail what had occurred since her arrival in London, with Richard adding a few comments of his own as they went. Theo and Fanny were amazed to hear that she was Lady Murray's granddaughter and shocked by her tale of imprisonment.

"Now we are married, I have taken up Frances' claim to her mother's estate," Richard continued. "It is not the money so much as the acknowledgement, reluctant or not, of the relationship."

Frances nodded in agreement. "As a matter of fact, we have just heard today that Lady Murray will agree that I am her granddaughter, though I expect we will never be close!"

"Do you think Lady Murray had anything to do with the attack on you?" asked Theo now, "Are you certain you were the target, or was it Frances?"

"I cannot think it," answered Frances. "How would she have contrived to meet the Comte and arrange such a thing? She scarcely leaves the house. It is not as if he were a relative or even a servant to entrust such a task to."

"No indeed," murmured Theo. They were obliged to end their conversation there as the rest of the guests began to arrive.

CHAPTER 36

R ichard went out to welcome the new arrivals and introduced them gracefully to Frances without making any reference to her past other than to say she had been living abroad and had only recently arrived in London. He wanted to see if anyone recognised her as Peter Francis, if not, he was tempted to let the deception pass unconfessed. Jack Lambert and Harry Belmont both gave her a second look, a slight frown on their faces. Sammy Fairfax however, immediately identified her as Diana from the Dalrymple's masked ball, and Carleton took the opportunity to tell them the shortened story of her relationship to Lady Murray and the disputed inheritance.

This caused Jack Lambert to study her even more closely as he recalled his encounter with 'Diana'. He stopped and stared at her in dismay as he remembered their conversation, good God, she had told him to his face that she was an adventuress, did Carleton know? He glanced sideways at him, but as he could see nothing in his face apart from an expression of polite interest, he schooled himself to patience, he could hardly quiz him in the middle of a dinner party.

His thoughts continued to race along, when he first saw Frances this evening he had imagined she looked familiar but Diana had been masked, he had not seen her face, it must be someone else that she resembled. It fretted him all through the first course, but it was Harry who inquired courteously, "Pardon me Lady Carleton, but do you have a young relative called Peter Francis? I have been wondering who you remind me of, the resemblance is quite striking."

Of course, thought Jack, Peter Francis was who she reminded him of, it was really quite a strong likeness, in fact ... he got a sudden cold feeling in the pit of his stomach and his eyes flew to Richard's. Richard held his gaze steadily, a slightly defiant look on his face. He folded his napkin deliberately and placed it on the table, then stood up and went to stand behind his wife, a hand resting lightly on her shoulder. "I think perhaps we had better tell our friends the truth, Frances. I was hoping we could finish dinner first but I think Jack has already guessed."

Frances glanced quickly up at Richard then looked directly at Jack Lambert, "You have guessed correctly, Mr Lambert," she said. "When I arrived in London and was searching for my identity I was masquerading for a while as Peter Francis." There were shocked looks on every face except for Theo and Fanny who looked at Richard in distress.

Frances continued matter-of-factly, "I was quite safe believe me, much safer than I would have been as a young woman alone in London, accompanied only by a manservant. I put up at the Pelican inn with John Hopgood to keep watch over me, and then

I accidently ran into Richard while he was being attacked by footpads and, well, the rest you have heard and here we are today!" She smiled brightly at everyone.

Jack Lambert looked as if he was biting his tongue to keep from exploding and Carleton spoke rapidly before anyone else, "I can assure you all, that although Frances has behaved unconventionally, she has done nothing to be ashamed of. I remind you that she is my wife, please consider that before saying anything we will all regret."

He paused and looked around at them all. "We would very much like you to remain our friends, but if you feel I am asking too much, then you must do as you see fit." There was an uncomfortable silence, Jack and Harry were both staring at Frances, finding their eyes drawn involuntarily to her breasts and figure as they struggled to come to terms with the fact that Frances and Peter were the same person. The others looked awkwardly from one to another.

Then, "I can't believe it!" blurted Harry, "Outshot by a girl!" The naive protest caused a burst of laughter from Jack and Richard and broke the tension between them.

"Come on, Richard, tell us the rest of the story," demanded Jack, "You can't leave it at that! How did you find out?" Carleton could not help himself, he blushed.

Frances leapt in with a smile to fill the silence as Jack stared at him, "I told Richard myself, I felt too guilty for deceiving him. Let me tell you a little more about what happened when I went to stay with my grandmother."

She kept them distracted for the next few minutes with the story of her imprisonment and rescue by Carleton, and then absorbed their full attention with her account of their runaway marriage by special licence, once again sending up a silent prayer of gratitude for Mrs Pearson's company on the journey which made it sound romantic rather than scandalous.

Jack sat back gratefully, he had not meant to embarrass Richard and he really did not want to know if Richard had made a pass at Peter. He thought he was the only one there with enough worldly knowledge to suspect that might have occurred. Hastily he poured himself another glass of wine.

The servants brought in the next course and everyone resumed eating, almost without realising that the moment to walk out had passed.

Later that night as they slid into bed, Frances told him contentedly, "Perhaps I will never receive a voucher for Almack's, but I think we have a wonderful group of friends who will stand by us. I am looking forward to arranging some house parties when we return to Chatswood, perhaps Harry and I can have another shooting match!"

"Yes indeed," agreed Richard distractedly.

"But?" queried Frances.

"Nothing important," he denied, unconvincingly.

"Richard, please tell me what is worrying you," she turned her head to look him in the eyes.

"It's only ... I think Jack thinks I ..." he trailed off and dropped his eyes, how could he explain that to his wife?

Frances reached out and held his face firmly between her hands, "You are right, it is not important. I know you love me whether I am Frances ... or Peter!" Carleton flinched. "Peter is still me, just me in different clothes, that is all. You don't need to worry what Jack thinks, or anyone else for that matter!"

She pulled him over so that his long, hard body was on top of her and kissed his mouth. "I love you so much, make love to me, Richard." In less than a second, all thoughts of anyone else except Frances had left his head.

EPILOGUE

Tom waited grudgingly for my lady's mysterious visitor to leave by the kitchen door. The man was wrapped in a black cloak, the hood pulled low over his face to conceal his features. Mr Hanson himself had let the man in, Tom not being considered responsible enough for that task, but Mr Hanson had decided it was acceptable for Tom to be the one to stay up late so that he could let the visitor out.

The man hurried down the lane, almost running. Tom looked after him and frowned, queer goings on and no mistake. He shut the door and made certain it was locked securely for the night. He had just turned away, ready to seek his bed again, when a piercing shriek split the air. For a moment he froze, his head swivelling, trying to decide if the sound had come from inside the house or outside in the street. A second scream convinced him it was coming from the first floor. Pausing only to grasp a stout stick from the collection beside the fireplace, Tom raced upstairs.

A scene of mayhem met his eyes. Annie, the maid, was backing out of the doorway into Lady Murray's sitting room, her apron over her face, her screams now reduced to whimpers. "My lady, oh, my lady!"

Tom pushed past her to find Lady Murray crumpled on the floor, her head covered with blood!

"Quickly," he told Annie, "Run and get Mr Hanson." He looked around, "Where is Miss Pettigrew? Her companion?"

They stared at each other in horror for a moment, each wondering if she had been struck down as well. Luckily for their jangled nerves, Miss Pettigrew appeared, tying a voluminous robe around her waist, her cap on her head. "Whatever is the matter, Annie?" she asked querulously.

Annie pointed a trembling finger into the room, "I came down to put 'er to bed and she wasn't in 'er room so I went looking for 'er, and there she is, on the floor! Murdered!"

"Nonsense!" said Miss Pettigrew automatically. However when she saw her mistress lying still, on the carpet, she was a little less certain. Very gingerly she knelt down beside her and touched her shoulder. "My Lady?" There was no answer.

By then the butler appeared, roused by all the commotion, hastily dressed in trousers and a coat which had evidently been chosen at random. "Has anyone gone for the doctor?" he asked sensibly, and then proceeded to send Tom off immediately on that errand. "Let's get her on the sofa," he decided, "It isn't seemly to leave her there on the floor." He looked to the two women for help to lift his mistress.

"Wait, let me get a cloth first, she won't want to get blood on the material, 'tis new," Miss Pettigrew objected. Then she realised Lady Murray might well be past worrying about such things. She plucked a small cushion from a nearby chair and placed it on the sofa. "That will do."

Together Annie and Hanson lifted Lady Murray off the floor onto the sofa and Miss Pettigrew sat down beside her, gently wiping the blood away with her handkerchief. "What happened?" she asked the butler fearfully, "Who has done this dreadful deed?"

For the first time, Hanson realised that he had most likely let a murderer into the house. He felt quite faint at the thought, should he call a constable? He wished Tom would return soon with the doctor, a medical man would likely know what to do, and besides, perhaps there was still some hope for his mistress.

It seemed hours before the doctor arrived, bustling in with his bag and hoping audibly that he had not been brought out on a fool's errand. As soon as he saw Lady Murray however, he cast a sharp look at Hanson, "What's been happening here?"

"I don't know, sir. Annie found her on the floor, like that. Is she ... dead, sir?" he asked anxiously.

Dr Everard was already bending down over the still figure. He looked up gravely at the hovering servants, and shook his head. "I'm afraid she's gone."

"She's been murdered! I knew it as soon as I saw 'er!" Annie exclaimed.

"I'm afraid she could be right," the doctor addressed Hanson as the senior man present. "Someone will have to fetch a constable."

Tom sighed, he knew full well who would be given that task!

It was Mr Adams who broke the news to Lord Carleton later the next day, still puffing slightly from his hurry to get there.

"Murdered!" Carleton echoed in disbelief. "Just a moment, Frances will need to hear this." He sent Rawlings off to ask her and Mrs Pearson to join them in the study as soon as possible. He waited impatiently for them to be seated, then invited Adams to continue.

"I have grave news, Lady Carleton. Your grandmother, Lady Murray, was found dead in her house last night. It troubles me to tell you this, ladies, but she was murdered, brutally murdered in her own sitting room!"

Mrs Pearson gave a small whimper of distress and buried her face in her apron. Frances stared wide-eyed from one man to the other. "Can this be true?" she asked.

Mr Adams nodded, "I am afraid so, I have already been down to Bow Street to confirm the news. I expect you will receive a visit from the magistrate in charge within a day or so, my lord, you and your wife being her next of kin."

He paused for a moment to give Carleton a meaningful look. "There is one more thing you should know, my lord. It appears that Mr Pilkington, Lady Murray's solicitor, cannot be found. It seems he has disappeared! Very suspicious, given the circumstances if I might say so!"

Carleton whistled. He found himself in full agreement.

Adams continued, "Once he heard I was your man of business, my lord, the magistrate, Mr Pringle that is, requested my assistance. He asked if I could help the constables search through the papers in Pilkington's office, to try and determine the motive for the attack. We start this afternoon, if I have your permission, my lord."

"Certainly, an excellent idea. I would appreciate it if you kept me informed of your progress."

"Of course, my lord." Mr Adams bowed and took his leave shortly afterwards.

"I never liked her, Richard, but I didn't wish this on her!" exclaimed Frances, and went into his arms.

A week later found them all once more gathered together in the study to listen to grave news from a visitor, but on this occasion the caller was none other than Squire Herbert, up from Selby for the week. After exchanging a few brief courtesies, the Squire got down to business, as eager to tell them his story as Lord and Lady Carleton were to hear it.

"You will be amazed at what news I have for you! Not only do we have the motive for your grandmother's murder, but we also know why the so-called Comte Duverne tried to kill you, my lady," he said with an air of satisfaction. His listeners stared at him with proper expressions of astonishment, although Frances was already leaping ahead in her imagination.

"So-called Comte Duverne?" queried Carleton.

The Squire nodded vigorously. "It seems there is no such person as the Comte Duverne. You will never guess who the pretender was!"

"No, tell us please!" entreated Frances.

"A French assassin! Apparently he found that masquerading as a Comte got him access into all sorts of places he would never been allowed into as plain Mr Duverne." Squire Herbert was well satisfied with the reaction this brought.

"It was as an assassin that he was hired by the solicitor," he continued. "It appears Pilkington sought him out through his underworld connections, the moment he discovered you had Lord Carleton's support, my lady."

Frances reached out to clasp Carleton's hand, but didn't interrupt.

"You will be glad to hear that Pilkington has been caught at Dover, attempting to escape over to France. He had some of Lady Murray's jewellery on his person, so there is no doubt he will hang for her murder. Once he knew there was no escape, he spoke freely, boasting of the fact that he had hired Duverne to assassinate you, Lady Carleton; Lady Murray knew nothing about it."

Frances and Carleton exchanged glances, no doubt Duverne had seen it as an extra bonus when he found the 'boy' he was seeking and his target were one and the same.

The Squire frowned uneasily at Frances. "The unfortunate truth is that both Pilkington and your grandmother have been stealing from your inheritance, my lady. When Pilkington found Bow Street was getting too close to him, he went to see Lady Murray. Apparently he had the gall to demand she provide him with the funds to escape, in return for his arranging Duverne's attack on you. However, instead of being grateful to him you will be glad to hear, she threatened to turn him in to the constable! They struggled when he tried to take her jewels and she fell and hit her head on the table. He says he didn't mean to kill her but that will make no difference, he will still hang for it."

"Serve him right!" exclaimed Frances. "I am exceedingly glad to hear that my grandmother was not part of the plot against me. I will try and think of her more kindly now, despite our differences."

The Squire took his leave a short time later, leaving the couple to mull over the news in private. He feared there would be much to do, to set Lady Carleton's affairs in order during the coming weeks. He did not think it necessary to tell Frances that Pilkington had claimed Lady Murray had been more upset about his demand for money, than the botched attempt on her granddaughter's life.

Let Frances think the best she could of her grandmother, it was a harmless deceit.

9 781930 112360